I0762217

THE VIOLENCE ALMANAC

THE VIOLENCE ALMANAC

MIAH JEFFRA

www.blacklawrence.com

Executive Editor: Diane Goettel
Book and Cover Design: Zoe Norvell
Cover Art: "Hard Determinism, Series 20 #34" by Heather Goodwind

ISBN: 978-1-62557-141-0

Published 2021 by Black Lawrence Press.

For Randall, fly where you want to fly.

TABLE OF CONTENTS

The drops of rain make a hole in the stone,
not by violence, but by oft falling.
—Lucretius

If they come for me in the morning,
they will come for you in the night.
—Angela Davis

FOREWORD: GROWL

The rumble comes from deep in the throat, a low place, breath slow and soaked in the shaping of sound, a snarled pranayama, the chords fold and judder, their own capricious Ring of Fire. We never expect it. Our lips pull up in the way that we signal disgust, or mimic singing a Mötley Crüe song, our nostrils spread open in the scrunch, and the teeth, the canines specifically reveal themselves in the snarl. And the sound of gravel, of rumble, of some force coming. *Growl.* We can't even say the word without yielding effort, a full commitment of the mouth to convey the idea. A full, open-wide presence. *We are predators,* this sound speaks. But what does that mean?

My first memory of it is what one would expect: a dog. A hound. A long slate gray snout that juts from sagged eyes. A military housing playground in Norfolk, Virginia. I am six. I stand in front of the dog, this creature that appears so snug in the hub of civility, yet a beast. An animal. What makes this one different from the wolf or the bear? My six year-old genius suspects once peering into the dog, the mystery of this animal will soon be discovered. I stare, committed to the science, my elliptical reflection in the black glass of its droopy eyes. And then it comes, the slow rising rumble, the quivering of slack lip, the teeth, and before I reason enough with my instincts to retreat, the whole mouth upon me, a soft bite, more of a warning than an attack. But the impression holds vivid, not so much the bite but the sound. *Don't fuck with me*, this growl says.

My mother's growl is wild and screeching and involves a frying pan in our trailer park kitchen. She, in a bathrobe. Her second husband, my stepfather, in his threadbare underwear. The smell of eggs overcooking, garlic and farts. He swarms her with accusations that don't possess much specificity, that grow more abstract with their frequency: *Where were you?* and *You should* and *Answer me*. My mother's auburn hair crackles dry and electric, knotted on her head, some grabbing down her back and shoulders, Autumn straw sprung sideways, reaching out. Bill's litany grows more confident with my mother's silence, more cracking, more adolescent. "You, you, me, you, me, you, you, bitch, you, bitch, me, me, me" and then it emerges: the low rumble, grumble in the throat, the lips, the teeth, and then further, something even more, the rise into a shriek, high in the head and splayed out in three-dimensional space, a noxious sound. And the frying pan, from stove to my stepfather's shoulder, his mouth a big stupid O, my mother's mouth a rack of violence, eggs arcing through the air, steam rising from the fury and the food. *Don't fuck with me*, this growl says.

The growl of our stomachs. We hear it, and we think it tells us we hunger. In fact, that is not the case. Our stomachs, our intestines, ceaselessly serve to push, to send things from our mouths to our assholes. It is a loyal and perpetual labor. Smooth muscle contracts in waves, steers the stuff, perhaps fried eggs, through twenty-five feet of coil. It is always happening, every moment, but we only hear it when our guts are empty. That is when the sound reverberates from inside, suddenly played in an amphitheater for its effort. It is then that we understand the want of the thing. It is an echo of need.

I am fucking a boy in Los Angeles, California. We are in the back seat of my car in the parking structure of Amoeba Records. I meet him in the used CD aisles, between Depeche Mode and Earth, Wind and Fire. It was in the middle of one of many slutty Hollywood interludes. A bell of sweat drops from my nose onto his barely there chest, smooth muscle, his tiny brown nipples, and then he makes the sound. The growl, teeth and all, eyes fixed. He is telling me, no warning me: I am an animal. You are a beast. We are all and only nature in this cramped capsule of pleather and plastic and metal and glass. It works. I get harder than I already am, yet am so hesitant of the hunger—so not as present, in my ambivalence—that I can only giggle, watching my body disappear and reappear into his own, this fleeting boy. *Fuck me*, this growl says.

Growls suppose an incivility. It is up there with ass-picking and hocking snot. We never expect it from ourselves. We *tsk tsk*, we denounce, we condemn its bestial origin, and yet our pupils come alive, a light in our moment, our bodies sweat, get wet, get hard, get sprung. What else does it remind us of? Are we not most beast when immediate? Don't we always move from mouth to asshole? And isn't it us being our most civil selves, to give warning to our violence, before the bite, before the strike, before the demand to love?

There are people growling everywhere. At any given moment, there must be thousands of growls. A child in Yucaipa howls at her brother—that's *my* fruit-roll-up. *My precious.* A tow-truck driver in Oakland knows the roommate is gone, and the roommate's girlfriend has made it very clear that the coast is too with a condom in her teeth, a snarl of its own kind. Every day, there must be nurses, husbands, schoolchildren, baristas, carpenters, parking meter attendants, dog walkers, born-again Christians, vapor clerks that find their paws and claws, their rumble, in the folds of civility. Fathers alone must account for so many growls, the muddle of safeguard and violence so braided in their boyhood. And then there is Angela Cavallo, who lifts a 1964 Chevy Impala to save her teenage son, pinned underneath its metal and glass. Imagine *that* growl, that echo of need so strong it rattles in the chamber of every heart.

Every time a promise is taken, a promise needs shielding, a promise is about to be fulfilled. An about to, an about to. It's all in the about to happen that we erupt, these growls, these warnings of our immense power; how often, open-wide, we echo in need.

BABIES

"I was big, Paul D, and deep and wide and when I stretched my arms all my children could get in between. I was that wide."

—Toni Morrison, Beloved

FLOATING SIGNIFIERS

"What's wrong with Mary?" Noah asks, his large brown eyes peering beyond his mother at the bathtub, his feet on tip-toes, a single Cheerio stuck to his left cheek. He shifts his feet, looks behind him, then back at the tub. "Can she swim?" He already knows this question will not be answered. He knows it's not a good question. It doesn't feel good to ask it. He pinches and pulls on his ear. He doesn't know why exactly, but he thinks that he shouldn't look directly at his mother. She is on her knees in front of the bathtub. She is still, quiet, her straight brown hair hiding her face, like it does all the time. He looks back to his baby sister Mary, who has her face down in the water. There isn't a lot of water in the tub, but she is kind of floating, and doesn't move. He grips the sides of the door moulding, and looks behind him again. He thinks it might be good to get out of here, let his mother and Mary be alone, like he shouldn't be here, like he walked into a place he should never be. And, right now, he should be outside, maybe climbing the Ash tree in the front yard, maybe going up near the top where the leaves are thick and where no one can see him. But Mary isn't moving, and his mother isn't, either, and it makes him not move, too, and it makes him feel like he's stuck in mud, and it upsets him. He begins to tear up.

"Mommy?" And he knows he shouldn't say her name, especially with tears in his eyes, and that he should run to the tree and climb as high as he can, but he's not sure what else to do.

"Come here, Noah," says his mother, her back to him, still facing the bathtub, where Mary is floating and not moving.

Noah doesn't move. He's afraid to go to her, but he's also afraid to not listen. He flexes his fingers on the door moulding. The tears get hotter. "Mommy?"

"Come here, Noah," says his mother, still facing the bathtub, her voice soft, maybe a little tired, which confuses Noah. She doesn't seem angry with him for not listening, doesn't seem angry about Mary floating in the water, not moving. But he still feels afraid to get closer, and afraid to move. Maybe Mary is afraid to move, too.

"What's wrong with Mary?" Noah asks again. This time, his mother turns around to look at him, and he sees her face, and it's not angry, and it's not upset or crying. But it's scary. It looks like nothing at all.

He runs, to go to his room, where he can shut the door, where he can close out his mother's face until she gets better or until his father gets home, until someone else comes into the house. He hears her footsteps behind him. She is running, too. She is chasing him, but not like the way they play tag, where they will run around, him and his brothers, in the front yard, laughing, and she will say, "I'm gonna get ya", and scoop him up in her arms and tickle him until he almost pees his pants, wetting his cheeks with loud kisses. She is not saying anything, and he only hears her footsteps, and he knows he can't let her catch him. He is almost at the door when he remembers: the Ash tree. She won't be able to catch him in the tree, and he can climb up to the top, and hide in the leaves, and wait until someone comes to the house, and can make everything better.

He turns back, but she is there, and her arms are out, and he feels confused, and looks back at the bedroom door, but knows he has to try to get to the tree, because she can't catch him there. So he balls his fists, and puts on his mean face, because he knows he's going to have to run down the hall right towards her if he wants to get outside, to get to the tree, and he pretends the Ash tree is calling him, Red Rover, Red Rover, send Noah over, and he runs, and he sees her arms grabbing for him. They are on his shoulders, his waist, his head. But he gets through, and he is running towards the door, and the little window by the door shows the tree outside, the leaves thick and green in the summer, that will hide him all day. He is opening the door, and can see the crack of light flood into the room from behind the big heavy door, and then he feels her arms wrap around his waist, and they pull. His hand loses the doorknob.

Noah screams. He screams, "No, Mommy!" She is dragging him backward, back to the bathroom, back to the tub, where Mary is floating and not moving. He tries to grab anything on the way, the armchair, the wall, a picture frame, and then the light of the bathroom is bright and yellow. He tries to hurt her, just a little, scratches at her arm, but he can't do much, and it's his mother so he doesn't want to.

She grabs the back of his neck, and he is surprised by how strong his mother is, by how much it hurts, and he turns to tell her, that she's hurting him, and he sees her face, and it's red and blotchy like it gets when she chases him and his brothers in the yard, when they play tag, but it is still not angry or upset, and it still looks like a nothing face, and that makes his tears even hotter.

"It's time," she says, and his mother forces his head forward, and he feels the water on his face. It is warm. He closes his eyes so they don't sting in the water, but he forgets to close his mouth and all the water comes in, and he tries to pull up so he can cough it out but his mother's hand is really strong. He tries to cry out for his mother, to help him, and he swallows more water, and his chest hurts really bad and he can't breathe. He opens his eyes, and Noah sees Mary, her arms over her head like she is flying, her thin hairs blowing all around in the water, and it's like air, like she is flying above him, and he is at the top of the Ash tree, and she can't see him, either, even though she's flying above him, her little hands really puffy, her face really puffy, her little nose, her eyes open, her mouth open, her little nose.

SIGNIFIER OF THE SIGNIFIER

The biographer highlights words, simple words, in the document, looks up synonyms in the online thesaurus: agony becomes anguish, sadness becomes desolation. Motherhood. What else can motherhood be? Guardianship? Too clinical. Custody? Too...small. Motherhood seems to reach in all directions, she thinks, the rays of a sun, the arms of Vishnu. Does the word fit in this context? She slides her fingers around the stem of her glass, pulls the California wine to her California lips, feeling the sophistication of the gesture in her hand, her slender shoulders, and stares at the word, flickering on the computer screen. She sighs, as that is what one would do, contemplating a manuscript in the night with a glass of red wine cupped close to the face. If she were feeling more confident about her process, she might betray the moment with a giggle, laughing at herself.

Should a mother, a mother in motherhood, ever be so conscious? Or, should she be more so, absolutely?

The biographer is a mother. Perhaps that is what drew her to this book project, this profile of Andrea Yates, of an act so forbidden even her writer self would never indulge on the page. Maybe that is exactly why she agreed to the book—it gave her permission. Now, the publisher asks her to write this story for a fascinated and horrified audience, for a craving audience. Tell this story. People want to read it. When one craves, they desire a thing inside of them, to enter their bodies, to eat it. Consume. That's the word.

The project allows the biographer to recall memories of her son, in moments she chose to bury. As a baby, when he cried all through the night, and in her exhaustion she entertained smothering him with the pillow. Or, when he screamed at her for taking him out of the toy aisle at Target, and all she wanted to do was slam the yellow dump-truck into his face. When she caught him smoking pot in the garage, and in his pubescent and insular torture he told her to "fuck off". How the flames in her eyes wanted to burn everything in her periphery. At that moment. Just for a moment. But, a moment, nonetheless.

The biographer sets the glass down and assumes the upright writerly position, her fingers hovering above the keys, and asks herself the same question: should Andrea be slovenly and unaware, a mousey, self-loathing woman who let herself go? Why does she feel the need to remind herself of this question? What is she trying to affirm? She glances at the corkboard above her desk, at the mug-shot photos of Andrea, the orange jumpsuit, the glasses, the flimsy straight hair that falls flatly against her face, the impotent bangs flopped on her forehead, all her features downward. The biographer wishes that she hadn't given up smoking, because she thinks it would be so, so nice to light one up and let the smoke dance around her fingers, delicately twisted as if to illustrate her present resolve of this particular scene, her indecision with how to paint the image of this woman, this monster, this woman, this mother. She instead takes a sip of her wine. There is a complexity here that defies law and trial. She imagines the Yates children in the back room, laid out on the bed, the wetness of the bathtub still clinging to their hair and soaking through the thin white sheet that covers them, and Andrea at the phone in the kitchen, quietly calling her husband. She imagines Andrea's hands folded in her lap, her knees turned in, like a child knowing she's about to be punished. Would it look like that? Would she possess this kind of unconscious reflection? Which Andrea would she be as she made that call?

Religious fanatic? Exhausted mother?

The biographer takes a large gulp of the wine absently, highlights "unconscious" and looks it up in the thesaurus. She selects "unwitting" and replaces it. Yeah, that's better.

SIGNS, SIGNS, EVERYWHERE THERE'S SIGNS

Andrea wakes up to the sounds of husband Rusty clomping his big feet on the floor of their room. "Andi, have you seen my belt?" She does not answer. Her dream still lingers, and she holds on to it, of her flying high above the ground, high above their small house, high above Houston, where she can just see the curvature of the earth, that great big ball of green and brown.

Rusty sits down on the bed beside her. He asks, "How are you feeling?" She only nods slowly, the weight of her head in this waking world so heavy, made of lead, her whole body, made of lead. She stares at the comforter, and into the already fading impressions of her dream, of the crisp air blowing briskly around her face. Rusty pats her thigh. "I've already fed the kids; they're in the kitchen." He gets up and walks over to the dresser, jerking open drawers, shuffling their contents. "That belt's gotta be around here somewhere. I just wore it yesterday. You know, the brown one, Andi?"

She shakes her head at the comforter.

"It's gotta be in this room. You didn't do anything with it, did you?"

You know, the brown one? Maybe you picked it up, not thinking, or something. Does that ring a bell at all?"

She shakes her head, the last bit of that huge Texas horizon leaving her memory now, the soft curve of the otherwise flat land gleaming along its edge from the clean yellow light of the morning. She thinks this is what astronauts must see when they come back to earth from a far-off mission. She wants to ask Rusty if he has ever seen pictures of this, maybe some of his co-workers at NASA collect these types of pictures, arrange them in neat black lacquer frames, and hang them all over their houses. She would like to see some of them. Wouldn't it be nice if Rusty asked them for a picture or two, to hang in her own house, in a frame.

The children make their usual erratic sounds from down the hall: laughing, raising their voices to best the others, all talking at once. She hears one say, "That's my Cheerio!" It's Luke, newly versed in what is his and what isn't, what is mine and what isn't. There is some clinking of spoons and bowls, and Noah asserting his command as the eldest, with his new voice—one of reason. "There are more Cheerios, Luke. Let John have that one and I'll get you another. Jeez." Andrea closes her eyes, lets her head fall back. It annoys her when Noah uses words like "Jeez". What's more, it was probably she that said it first, that planted the seed, when she was in one of her moments, when the kids are all around her, Mary in her arms, John climbing on furniture, Luke yelling across the room, Matthew pulling on her pantleg, when she cannot commit to a single action, her body stuck, with so much of the world happening all around it. Rusty is now with them, because Andrea hears him say, "That's right. You want more, Luke?"

And then Rusty is back in the bedroom, his long torso and neck leaning forward, like the thick brow of his head was a searchlight leading the way for his stringbean body. He had such a nice frame, but his ducked posture, as if he was embarrassed by his height, somehow took the man out of him. "I still can't find that darn belt, can you believe it? I gotta be at work soon, and if I don't find that belt my pants may fall down. Can you imagine that, Andi?" He is not so much searching as merely shuffling things around, making noise. "Did you do laundry or something? Maybe I left it on my pants yesterday. You think maybe you washed the pants with the belt on? You think they're in the washer or something? Did you wash clothes yesterday?"

"No, Rusty."

"Alright. No biggie. I just can't find that belt. How does something just disappear like that? It was just here."

"Yes, it was."

"I guess I'll just have to hope that my pants don't fall down." Rusty laughs, tips his head back, glances at Andrea, the thin translucent sheet barely protecting her slender, yet softening, body. He moves to her, picks up her chin, kisses her gently on the lips. "You think you'll be all right until Mother comes?"

The smell of his breath—coffee and milk, and the faint onion that always lives in his mouth—makes her pull away, and she immediately wants to say sorry, for ruining the sweetness of the moment, but she doesn't feel strong enough to say it, and the smell. She hopes her lowered eyes will be the apology he needs, so he doesn't regret kissing her, so he doesn't regret loving her.

"Okay," he says, either ignoring the slight or not noticing. "Don't get into too much trouble. Mother will be here in about an hour."

Andrea musters a nod for this, she owes him that at least.

She listens for Rusty's good-byes to the kids, and for the inevitable slam of the front door—Rusty never notices how hard he handles things—and then sits in the bed in relative silence, her flimsy straight brown hair matted to her pale face. Noah is softly speaking from somewhere within the walls of the house, and she imagines Paul, who so adores Noah, gleaming up at him, and John trying to feed Luke something he shouldn't eat, a piece of hardened Texas mud caked on a sneaker, or a ball of lint, so he can hear him squeal, "yucky", and Mary in her crib on all fours, pushing to sit up. And all of this at once, and in the next moment something else altogether, and more and more talking and squealing and pushing and yelling and smacking and pulling and noise and energy. Savageness in them. And it's her fault, because she can't help but allow it all to happen. She can't wrap her arms around it all and keep it. One at a time is all she can manage. One at a time.

She slides off of the bed, fixes and smooths the comforter with her hand. She moves to the closet, pulls Rusty's belt from the bottom of a box of old winter sweaters, the smell of stale wool and cardboard, brings it to his dresser drawer, and drops it on top of his white athletic socks. She closes the drawer, careful that it stays open just a bit, the way he left it, walks out into the hallway, into the bathroom, and opens the faucet to the tub.

"Paul, honey. Mommy needs you."

OPPOSITIONAL READINGS

Seventy-five minutes after Rusty leaves for work he is back at home. He is on the front lawn, pounding the ground with his fist, the spit around his open mouth rubbed with grass and dirt. What is it about intolerable pain that forces our mouths to open? And why can't he close it, this simple action?

The cold in his stomach, creeping up to his armpits, made his hands shake on the steering wheel, even in the summer Texas heat, on this ride home. How many times had Andi said into the phone, "It's time. I did it. It's time," and how did he know what that meant? Why did he know what it meant, this cryptic mantra, so much so that he leapt out of his desk chair and ran down to his boss' office to ask to be excused? And if he did realize it, what did it mean that he left her with the kids, in any case? Was there something unusual about Andi this morning, something more unusual, something that he should have noticed? How did he have a wife—choose a wife—that he wouldn't notice when she was different in some way, in some very big way?

Rusty was flooded with images on that short drive home, but they were not of Andrea's "illness"—a diagnosis he did not believe real, a mere scam for doctors and pharmacists to bleed money out of their bank account, to prey on those that are not strong in their convictions, in their faith. What came to him instead were random moments: Andrea in the scrubs she wore when she worked at the hospital, swing dancing with a patient and laughing, her head tilted high, hair falling easily down her back; Andrea in her wedding dress, grinning during the vows as if the two of them were privy to a secret told only to them, her lips pink and glossy; Andrea running in the yard with the children, playing tag, the giggle-screams echoing off the other houses in the neighborhood; the milky smell of his daughter Mary's thin hair.

He always knew Andrea had doubt in her heart. This was normal for anyone in the faith, but he knew that what tortured her was knowing the truth yet being incapable of letting go of the doubt. And that's what one needed to do with doubt: let it go. Doubt was an addiction, one that we gripped, wrapped our fingers around, that felt more tangible than faith. Rusty tried to help her through it, to feel the truth for what it was, something just as real, that for some reason was much easier for him to hold. When he saw the truth fade from her, in moments of quiet, or in the car on the way to Church, or even at the dinner table—it spread across her face like an imperceptible bruise—he would immediately take her hand and pull her down to the floor, or pull the car over, and pray. Best to address these feelings of doubt at the moment they occur.

Rusty drove back home anxiously, biting the inside of his lip until it bled, but did not once exceed the speed limit.

The paramedics were already there. Their faces were all white as the wet sheet in the back room, even these men who dealt with the dead every day, with dead flesh every day, with blood, with eyes wide open staring into nothingness. The police would not let Rusty come into the house, but he could smell the feces, the vomit, the death from inside. He searched for her, a glimpse of her, this woman whom he married, had made a family with, whom he loved. He ran to the side window, to the back door, searching, and for one brief moment he caught a glimpse of her inside, her mousy brown hair stringy and gnarled around her deathly gray face. This is not the image he wanted to see. He immediately thought of that day when he took her to Glamour Shots in the mall, where they blow-dried and sprayed her hair, dressed her in that really nice jean jacket with the rhinestones on the collar, where they made up her face with rouge and pink lipstick. And the pose. She looked so confident, her chin pushed out, her eyes focused and full of ambition. She used to wear this pose every day, a woman so smart and quick and full of wonder for the world. She was the valedictorian of her high school! She was a dedicated nurse! She had everything it took to be the perfect partner in Christ, to be a perfect mother.

But then, she was gone. He couldn't see Andi, somewhere hidden, twisted in the angles of this house that he already hated. And Rusty screamed, "How could you do this?" It came out high-pitched, shrill. What startled him, upon raising the question was that he didn't know whom he was directing it toward.

"it is the supreme way to hurt my husband"—(Medea, 140-41)

ARGUMENT

She knew it was illegal and wrong. There were plenty of signs supporting that. She waited until her husband had gone to work so he would not stop her. She prepared. She was methodical. She called the police afterward. Her mental illness was not relevant. She had knowingly done it to escape a life she hated. She wanted to punish her husband. Luke had strands of his mother's hair clamped in his little fist. Here are the pajamas of her children, enter them into evidence. It shows how much smaller these children are than their mother. Yes, yes, take a look at this PowerPoint. It details psychosis at length. Yes, she may have been having delusions about harming her children, but what makes her sane is that she did nothing to protect her children from the delusions. Andrea herself even declared that she knew that what she did was a sin, and isn't that enough evidence that she is not insane? She covered the bodies with a sheet. Is that really the action of an insane person? The sheet signifies that she felt guilt. She kept the plan secret because she knew it was wrong. She also watched Law and Order, and saw the episode where a woman drowns her child in a bathtub. It inspired her. This gives her actions the quality of premeditation.

Now, let's be silent for three minutes, to experience the length of time each child endured the water, before dying.

(Excerpt of the screen adaptation of the biographer's hardback bestseller, Maniac Mother: Murder and the Medea Complex, but the Made-for-TV film is titled, simply, Maniac)

FADE IN:

A typical Houston lower-middle-class suburban street, sunny and quiet, no cars on the ambling street. Houses are painted white, beige, and brown. They are small, clean, a little run-down. Leaves green the tidy row of Ash trees lining every yard.

EXT. A FRONT YARD – DAY.

A tricycle lies upside-down on its handlebars, its front wheel spinning.

NOAH sits under the Ash tree, looks up into its leaves, the sun peeks through in small moments. NOAH looks at the small beige house with worry.

INT. A BEDROOM – SAME.

RUSTY paces at the foot of the bed. ANDREA sits in the bed, blankets around her. She holds her stomach. Her thin brown hair is a tangled, twisted mess around her face.

ANDREA

I can't, Rusty. I don't know…

RUSTY

Andi, it's a blessing.

ANDREA

Of course it is. But, I don't know…

RUSTY

Maybe it'll be a girl. You've always wanted a girl.

ANDREA

Yes. It's…so much.

RUSTY

Can you imagine if it was a boy? Another one? Five in a row? What are the odds? No, it'll be a girl. We can name her Mary. Wouldn't that be nice?

ANDREA

After Magdalene.

RUSTY

No. Of course not. The Virgin Mother.

ANDREA

But what about the boys? It's so much. I feel like I can't even take care of them, the way we are meant to. You know?

RUSTY

The boys are fine, Andi. They're doing good. And, I'll be there. I'll help you.

ANDREA

But when you're not around, sometimes, I get these awful thoughts, like I'm doing something terribly wrong, like I'm… poisoning them.

RUSTY

Don't be so hard on yourself. Why are you saying these things? It's a baby. It's a blessing.

ANDREA

Yes. Yes, Rusty.

RUSTY

It is our duty, isn't it? And God has given us such fertility for a reason. To spread love, to spread faith.

ANDREA

You make it sound like they are the same thing.

RUSTY

What?

ANDREA

Love and faith, like they're the same thing.

RUSTY

Well, they are. If you give your life to God, fully.

ANDREA

No, Rusty, that's where you're wrong.

RUSTY

Andi, what is this?

ANDREA

Sometimes, when I'm playing with the boys in the front yard, and we're laughing and running, and I stop to rest because my body can't keep up with them, my heart bursts with this overwhelming feeling of love. They laugh like angels. And then, a second later, my chest gets cold, and a terror comes into me. I can't keep them safe. I'm winded from running for a few minutes, Rusty, and I can't go further, and I couldn't protect them at that moment, if they needed me. At many moments. My faith in God, it disappears whenever I feel…the most love for the boys.

RUSTY

Andi, I don't understand this weakness in you.

ANDREA

I don't think it's a good idea, Rusty.

RUSTY

What are you implying?

ANDREA

The doctors said it is inadvisable. It's…I might get worse.

RUSTY

The doctors?! What do they know about our life? About what's important? If I didn't know better, I'd think you were falling into their trap, Andi. Doctors. There is no morality in doctors. Were you suggesting we…not have the baby? What kind of evil has come into you? The doctors.

LUKE, 2 years old, comes into the bedroom, pinching his penis through his cotton pajamas.

LUKE

I gotta pee-pee, Mommy.

RUSTY grabs LUKE, a little harshly, by the shoulders, turns him directly towards ANDREA.

RUSTY

You see this child? This beautiful, sweet boy? What? If you would have listened to the doctors, he wouldn't be here.

LUKE

Ow, Daddy.

ANDREA

Rusty. Stop.

RUSTY

What has come into you? Don't you see what poison they're feeding you? How can you be like this, Andi?

LUKE

(whimpering)

Daddy.

RUSTY

We are not on this Earth to listen to doctors. You have a duty, as a mother, as a woman.

ANDREA

Stop it, Rusty! You're hurting him.

RUSTY

Hurting him?! You're talking about something far worse.

ANDREA

(crying)

Stop it!

RUSTY

Don't you want your children to live?

LUKE quietly sobs, while his pajamas slowly darken as he wets himself.

"I loved to swim. I used to see how many summersaults I could do underwater with one breath."

—"Noah", on the site yateskids.org

DRAGON-PULLED CHARIOT

The biographer sits at her desk. She is drunk off of her California wine, her eyes watery smudges. There is an open notebook, and there is a pen laying, lying on the blank page. She has recently become prone to sitting here not to write, but to stare out the window, to look into the moments that occurred before, to recall the writing. How did it come, exactly? How did she fill pages, then fill bookshelves, then fill theatre seats, when she knew no more about Andrea than when she had begun? Andrea. Maniac Mother. That title was the publisher's choice. What else had been? The publisher told her, this is your story. Take liberties. This is your story. And now, that story is being read. Being eaten. Consumed. But there was so much more the biographer had hoped for. She wanted to understand, not just Andrea, but the Andrea inside herself.

And what of children, like her own son, that grip women's insides, and tear the most tender of flesh to guarantee a first breath? How is it that women love such a thing, love it with a ferocity that mirrors the violence of its birth? There is a lot of vicious emotion in all of it, some kind of fury, and we know how fury moves: it shoots out in all directions with little control. And the intensity is more uncontrollable, more powerful, the closer to the source. She wanted to understand.

So, they die. They can die. Who knows this more than the one that brought them life?

And what of the mother? She will cut her hair. She will file her nails. She will replace a hip. She will vomit. She has the right. When does an excising of the body warrant lament, like an unpleasant dream during a troubled sleep?

Perhaps Andrea did believe that her children were on their way to Hell. Maybe they were. Maybe there was no madness at all, but a clarity that presents itself the way light slices through gaps in curtains that sway with wind against a cracked window. Or maybe Andrea's own doubt was the gap, that her children would fall through, down into a life that terrified her. The fear consumed mothers well before Andrea, and perhaps they summoned their own stories and presented them to her in these folds of mania. Would they recommend a repeat of their own actions? Whatever happened to these mothers?

Medea ascended the sky like a set of stairs in a dragon-pulled chariot, some say of fire, into the heavens, her face twisted in both a grin and grimace, her hair like a fury, extending outward in every direction behind her, all volume and power.

Andrea went to jail.

What does it mean that the biographer has never believed in God, or the grace of God? How can she understand Andrea if she herself has never felt that pull towards anything divine? She thinks of her own son, imagines him with children of his own, wondering the exact same thing at a similar spot in his own home.

The biographer wanted to write this, all of this, but how would it have made sense? How would it have been understood? The publisher knew it wouldn't. The publisher implored the biographer: Make it more simple. Take liberties. For the sake of the reader. If Andrea is too human, the reader will be confused. All stories need a villain. Simplify.

The biographer looks over on her bookshelf, Maniac Mother. She sneers. The biographer knows this is not Andrea's story. It's not even hers. Why does that make her feel like scrubbing her fingers until they are raw? They now pull the wine glass to her lips.

The biographer sits at her desk and drinks. The biographer sits at her desk. The biographer sits. The biographer. She is eaten. Consumed.

What we don't expect
some god finds a way
to make it happen.
So with this story.

A CHAIR IS A CHAIR IS A CHAIR

Andrea sits in a polished wood chair. She wears black slacks, a blue-gray printed button-up and a white cardigan. Her glasses reflect the fluorescent lights of the courtroom, and disappear into her wilted brown hair. As the sentencing is read—life in prison, but spared the death penalty!—Andrea nods with small, jerky gestures, yes master, yes master. She turns to her attorney, a man with an astonishingly white and thick head of hair, a man who could have been a country star in the 80s, and smiles. She smiles perhaps at him, to say thank you for trying, or perhaps she is relieved. Or, something else.

She had to recount to so many strangers the specifics of the morning in the bathtub—as she thinks of it now—so many times: the where of it, the when of it, the what of it, the words spoken, the actions laid out in time, the moment and then the next, an almanac of violence. Now, as they read the details of her sentence, she thinks of it differently, the way she felt then. A cutting away, releasing the doubt, to preserve what good they had left in them. God would never damn a child to the abyss, she had reasoned then, but if she kept on to them, held them close in this world, her world, they would all fall into that gaping hole, the one of eternal torment, her doubt, her weakness. She had to cut them loose from her own fate. It was the only way.

But why not herself? Well, that is the question she wonders now. And, perhaps that is the guilt she will live with forever. Why not me?

There were many times, even as a child, where she felt the pull into this abyss, even when she hadn't a language for it. One time she clearly recalls, amidst the glare of the courtroom lights. She was with her mother at a discount department store, like a Target or Walmart, but neither of these. Her mother had just gotten in the cashier's line, her cartful of kitchenware and plastic knickknacks tumbled about in the chipped wire basket. Her mother, moments ago in the aisles laughing with her about boys—particularly Kevin Armstrong, the one with the round-rimmed glasses and the crush on Andrea—now appeared sad, staring ahead into nothing, all the lines in her fine face drawn down. Andrea, no more than eleven, looked to the left, to the other lines of filled up carts and men and women, some children, also staring blankly, straight ahead, some peering over to the magazine covers that wall-flowered the aisle. Then to the right, the same. They were simply waiting to buy their goods, and would probably be all right once they made it past the cashier, but Andrea could not push off the watery feeling of dread low in her belly. She loved people, found them marvelous and complex and fascinating, and this image of them blank and listless felt like a betrayal. And so, in came the dread like a hose filling a kiddie pool, swirling around the bottom of her gut. She isn't sure why she remembers at this moment—among the many, many times she felt this liquid weight, this particular memory—but here it is. It wasn't the first time she had felt it, and certainly wasn't the last time, or even a time she felt it more profoundly. Maybe it was the lights in the store, the fluorescent lights, much like the ones in the courtroom, that caught the thin film of sweat on the shoppers' foreheads, or maybe it was because she would get her period later that day for the first time.

Andrea never had a language for the way she felt in these moments—at the store, in a fast-food drive-through, at the airport, at the family dinner table—until Rusty. They were walking along McKinney Street on a pleasant spring afternoon, not far from where they met a few months prior, enjoying ice cream. It was then that she first shared those feelings, ambling beside women loaded with shopping bags. And very calmly, with no hesitation, Rusty said, "You were moving towards the devil." She hadn't thought of this. She hadn't thought much about the devil at all, or God, for that matter. All she really believed was wrapped up in people, the way they treated one another, what they thought about, how they lived. It never occurred to her that the dread came from anywhere beyond humanity. And then, there it was: the devil, which means there was also God. Rusty said the words, and just like that the whole idea appeared to her. And she felt guilty that she had not conceived of it before. So, just as she experienced her first moment of faith, so did she of guilt.

And now Andrea is sitting in this polished wood chair, and knows that in mere seconds she will be carried away, down into a series of hallways, one of them leading to her prison cell, a small square space with dark walls and a slat of a window, where the light will pierce instead of glow on her face. A photographer is snapping pictures of her. She looks out into the large courtroom, the cavernous ceilings, and allows herself to return to one of her favorite dreams, where she lifts off, rises into the air, through the roof, over buildings and freeways, cities and suburbs, and over Texas, the horizon slightly curving like the edges of waterlogged wood. And she flies over the home she grew up in, the rusting swing-set lodged crooked in the ground, her mother serving hot dogs on ridged and white paper plates, next to the horseshoe pit. And her home in Houston, and its small front yard with the Ash tree, the one Noah loves to climb into when the leaves go full bloom, and as she floats directly over the tree she sees, yes, she sees Noah, his small dark eyes, like a bird's, looking up into the sky, waiting for her to fly overhead, he hidden in the safety of the leaves.

But that is not what the people in the courtroom see, and it is not what millions of others see when this same picture is printed in Time, or the Washington Post, or on the internet when they Google her name late at night, many years later, ashamed of their own recurring fascination with this woman who murdered her five children. What they see is a woman staring blankly, a mother, staring straight ahead, into nothing.

Paul D: "Was it hard? I hope she didn't die hard."
Sethe: "Soft as cream. Being alive was the hard part."

JINGLE-JINGLE-POP

Champagne would have understood, I don't need no one telling me. She didn't take nothing personal, and she wouldn't want me getting all cry-baby and shit in front of the girls. Someone had to be mama bad for those pansy-ass chochas. And Champagne knew, knew that I was getting close, and to lose a day, lose an hour, would have been a setback. A *setback*. I was getting so close. Not just the money, but the whole thing, you know? What the head does. It's like what Donald Trump say in that show, you got to keep the *eye on the prize*. Champagne knew that, though she was a dumb bitch. That's what got her dead. She stopped looking the johnnie boys up and down, getting the real deal off them, and wound up popping her ass in any car that rolled by. Ooh, the money, it did that thing, you know. She was probably dying in that mother fucker's hands, knowing she bleeding all over, but her eyes went way outside the car window into that place where the promise was, probably smiling away at how soft the life beyond was going to be.

It's good I didn't go, for reals. By the time the girls got back from the funeral, I turned a whole day's worth of tricks. Sunday wasn't usually a good day, the johns at church with their familias, but with all the girls gone I got the whole spread. Easy bread. Champagne probably say it a better use of my time, I can almost hear her, give me a hi-five, "a T gotta do what she gotta do."

I see them at Benito's, the tiny taco shack in the warehouse parking lot at the corner of Las Palmas. The warehouse used to be a porno slinger, but now it some fancy artist studios. Benito's once be jamming, all those fat porno guys slopping it up, flirting with us, working their job and loving it, but those artists with their skinny ass jeans and beards walk sideways around the damned place, oh, they eat organic or some shit. Hey though, the shack got bunk for food, and that's embarrassing for any Mexican joint in L.A. But it was open all night and became the spot. The taquitos were greasy enough to slice through the cum in our mouths. Champagne and me used to come by between tricks and she would play this game. She shimmy up on the stool and lay her head on the counter like she be busted, it was so funny, and say "Where'd you be right now if not here?" and we'd take our turns saying the Bahamas or Paris or one of them hotels on the Sunset Strip, or some shit.

The girls were done up in black, all respectful and funeral like, but there was no hiding who they were—pencil skirts stuffed in the hips, stilettos, low slung blouses to the titty-nipple, fake eyelashes with crystals on the tips. Fantasia had a bird in her hair, brown as her skin, with white bubble eyes staring out, a whole damn bird. Now, what bitch can do that? They were muy glamoroso, popped up on the cracked red plastic stools, crossing their legs like it helping any, three of them in a row, looking like Elvira just blew up all over Hollywood. So the fuck what? Straight bitches are jealous we do it full out every day. They wish.

Cheilah, Fantasia and Mimi, and no Champagne. Something about them sitting on those stools without her made it feel real. I pretended to fix an eyelash, cuz I'm not crying in front of nobody, honey.

"It was nice, real pretty, all the flowers." Mimi, always trying to play like some elegant bitch, her hands all folded on her lap. She had to do something, being the age she be.

Cheilah touched the white lily in her platinum wig, too big for her face, big enough for her eyes. "I took one for my hair. That ain't against the religion or nothing, right?"

"Like you worried *that* gonna throw you in the fire, girl?"

"Ain't that right, honey."

"You should have been there, Lalo," Cheilah said, and I just looked at her.

"If I die, my best friend better be there," Mimi said, cleaning under her jeweled nails. Fucking Lee Press-On shit, but they look good in that cheap way.

Fantasia laughed all husky and warm. "Girl know she couldn't wait that long to have a jimmy up her mangina. Ain't that right, Lalo? How else all that shit gonna stay up in there? Them dookie-lips singing some big-time opera, you know it."

"Your heart probably fall right out that bitch if you didn't keep it all plugged up," Mimi said, her eyes not even leaving those janky-ass nails.

I just looked at Mimi with all the eat shit that I could, because I was saving my tongue for now, and we'd see about who be talking when I'm up out of this place, and she still dropping to her knees while I'm buying earrings on the QVC.

"Oh, hell, Mimi, like you all tight?" Fantasia said.

Cheilah rolled her eyes. "Serious, though, Lalo. It was nice. You should have been there."

I just said, "You know the motherfucker that did Champagne like that was a Carlos."

We all nodded, and Mm-hmm, and Uh-huh, and You know that's right, girl.

I looked out, past the girls, at the block—the parking lots, the boxy warehouses, the concrete, the trash in the gutters, the trash cans, the concrete. The L.A. sun just kind of sat there, no breeze, just dry, still, dead heat. All the stanky sweat from plastic backseats and fat-ass johnny boys. It was gonna be real tough on the Boulevard without Champagne. She was my girl, my family out here, no matter how dumb she be.

Cheilah found her on Lexington, behind the Circus Club. Cheilah was inside a john's car across the street, her face pressed against the window. She saw the whole damned thing, watched Champagne get pushed out of the car, and the motherfucker speed off.

"She just fell out, her arms and legs all like *this*, you know? Like a doll."

She'd been beaten to death. No knives, no wrenches, she hadn't even been raped. It was all fist on that sweet face. Only some crazy Down Low motherfucker would kill with a fist. A Carlos. Champagne wouldn't stick it in him, I'm sure of it, and that's what got her waxed. She would never use her jimmy, refused to, never wanted to be reminded it was there, and that's all a Carlos wanted. Jesus, nothing worse than a DL pansy chocha.

"I saw the car, though. We need to go to the police."

"And do what, Cheilah?" I asked her, tossing my hair—my real hair—back, looking high and mighty, the only one with any sense at all. Like the po-po ever give a shit.

We called 911, and didn't give our name. I told Fantasia she could move into the efficiency with me, which was an honor, taking my girl's place like that. Fair enough. Fantasia made me laugh, tried to keep things light, even though she be the dylan of the bunch, with her big teeth and linebacker shoulders. Girl so ugly it make me like her. Besides, I didn't want to pay for the efficiency by myself, not this late in the game. But when I got back to the pad, I couldn't throw none of Champagne's shit away. Every time I tried to touch her clothes, or makeup, or that chipped Wonder Woman coffee mug she loved so goddamned much I'd get that pit in the gut that's all empty-like but heavy at the same time, and hear her laughing like she at the other end of a tunnel. You think I'd be done with the crying, but I couldn't help it. "You dumb bitch, you dumb bitch,"

I said to nothing but the tore-up shag carpet.

Me and Champagne go way back, both sixteen when we started tricking out on the Boulevard. We were sweet meat, so good that the girls didn't mess with us, so long as we didn't steal their regulars. We upped the real estate. This was all back when the Yukon Diner was still open down the block, and we'd dress up like some real trade after the worknight was over, or after we done dancing at the club, like four in the A.M., and parade ourselves through the place, before we feel all beat down by the Boulevard. All those drunk WeHo faggots and their hags be woot-wooting telling us how fabulous we looked, the girls with their look of pure envy—half-lids and too-wide smiles—as we worked it in our strappies and fringe, God Damn we were something, and the juice still swishing in our asses. Such fools, honey. Such fools.

We'd do the twirl in the Yukon, go back to the efficiency, and count our money. We both saving for tits back then, because we knew we both better than the Boulevard, wanted to get them together, but we spent our fair share chasing the dragon, too, cuz sometimes you needed a little feel-good before the get-go. She more than me, though. I wanted nice tits. And honey, when we got them, we were unstoppable, the sexiest motherfucking Ts in the mix. Ah, the feeling of walking down the street, feeling them jiggle to my shimmy, it was one of the first moments I felt *right*, you know what I'm saying? Like some kind of snap in the crackle-pop. I loved when the johnnie boys would first open up my shirt, and see the woman on me. I would imagine when I no longer had to trick, would imagine my real man opening up my shirt like that, with love on his mind. Ooh, that feel right.

You bought these, baby, I'd say to the johnnie boys, and crush their face in between.

I'm not gonna say that getting my ass hiked was a calling. It was the only thing that I could find easy, and believe me honey, I looked. No one wanted a pre-op T working their cash register, and that paid shit next to the Boulevard on a good day. Besides, even if some straight job hired me, they wouldn't let me wear what I liked, and that's a problem. No one tell me what I can't put on this body, and it's a fine-ass body. I lost mi familia for this shit, so I ain't covering up these titties just to give some rotted fat-ass his midnight donuts. I earned these motherfuckers, and they're not the jacked up shit a bunch of these bitches settle for in some pendejo's dirty bathroom at half-price. I went to a clinic in Beverly Hills for these, straight up. White walls, clean waiting room, good magazine selection. Nice doctor, friendly eyes, sat me down proper for a *consultation.* And I did it right, nothing too big. And no doubt I got the best ones on the Boulevard. But I'm more than my tits. I got legs that make you wanna give up chicken your whole life, and a thick ass, so strong I can tuck my jimmy way back between my cheeks and hold it while I walk. And if they wanna see it, I lean way back and make it pop right out like a jack-in-the-box. Some of the boys really like that, and I'll do it for the dough. Wind me up, johnnie boy, *jingle-jingle-pop!* Such fools, honey.

The bus stops were the best places to go, the ones on the Boulevard between Orange and Las Palmas Streets, until the po-po started giving a shit and scaring the good johns away, trying to ass-lick the mayor, make the rents go up. I miss those boys. They would roll up in their Toyota Tercels and Honda Civics, very reliable cars, fiddle with their wedding bands as we talked rate. They would look at you with appreciation, make you forget you just a cheap-ass T. They never argued the price, so willing to give tips. Yes, honey, everybody wants a steady man.

Nowadays, the clientele's not the same. It's not so simple and easy, no Murphys, no sweet-talkers. The Honda Civics come less and less, now they got Grindr and shit. Now, it's johnnies not so much afraid of the fuzz, but plenty afraid of what they are, so it's a whole different ballgame. They so fucked up they don't know they afraid, smelling like Tecate and all kinds of desperation, honey. We call them all Carlos. They be these pendejos all with wives and little niños running around in the yard, fixing cars and working construction jobs, muscles and big belt buckles and cowboy hats, but really they little faggots on the DL that want a big fucking jimmy up their ass. No shit. Champagne hated Carlos. They all skip work and go to this bar called Tempo, a fucking dump of a spot in a strip mall, down the street at Western, next to the Korean nail shop. You should see this place. You walk in, Tejano music blaring, and all the Carlos just standing there, all alone with their mustaches, pounding beer after beer. They get all worked up, glaring like animals on the hunt, but none of 'em say or do a damned thing to each other. Silent. They just keep drinking their beer until they get crazy fucked up and horny, and then they drive down the street, to us.

Shit gets more *unpleasant* with them, for sure, some rough fucking or a slap in the face here and there. Fantasia swear she hear them crying sometimes, but you never know seeing how hopped up she be on whatever she get her hands on. Cheilah said once that a Carlos was reciting the Hail Mary while she slipping him her jimmy, bent right over his back seat, and then he turned and slapped her right at the Amen. And that just wasn't my deal, oh no, but no Carlos ever did nothing crazy like what happened to Champagne. We just all knew they had it in them.

I started to T when I was fifteen, sneaking makeup and walking up and down Pacific Boulevard, pretending I was all Veronica Castro, the most glam bitch on Mami's telenovelas. So many cars showed their appreciation, and I was born to walk in heels. I swung my leg cross the other just enough to let the booty roll, and the horns would be honking. Child, that was the shit right then, feeling so tall and ready for it all. I would walk until just before dinnertime, slip through my bedroom window and tug off my sister's dress, wipe the makeup off, go back to being the boy I knew I really wasn't. I think Esperanza knew what I was doing but never said anything. She had to, sharing a room and all. I wasn't exactly a ghost, and the more I did it the more I owned it, started getting a little cocky feeling so good about myself, staying a little later and a little later.

Of course I was going to get caught, and maybe I wanted to, a little bit.

I went out on Pacific Avenue during Carnaval Primavera, and that was the end. It was risky, because my mami, sister, tía and that pendejo Alex my mother was talking about marrying were all out watching the parade. But so many people, I just couldn't help but get all dressed up, and I thought it would be easy to get lost in the crowd. I took one of Espie's dresses, the fuchsia one with the empire waist and sequined top that she wore at some dance thing she did. It felt just right draping on my hips, showing that little scoop where my ass hit my waist, just made for a man to rest his big hand. My legs were already getting long then, and even though my shoulders were not so thin anymore, I knew how to pull them back to look smaller. With some Wet n Wild on the lips and some of my mother's blue eyeshadow, I stepped out into the zoo of smiling people, looking fine. People looked at me, some woot-wooted, like I was part of the parade, and, honey, I floated, that was for sure. I moved the way I was supposed to—the swish and bootie—not that boxy, shoulders-down shuffle bullshit I had to fake so I wouldn't get my ass kicked. Huntington Park High School was no place for a woman like me. All the days of hiding beneath those dumb-ass baggy jeans and white t-shirts slipped away when the sun reflected off the sequins into my eyes, strutting down a sidewalk. As a boy, I was a sad looking thing, skinny and like I be sick. As a woman, I was Phoenix, I was Nefertiti, I was motherfuckin Xena. I was transformed.

But my mami recognized me. I didn't even have time to turn away before she be standing, out of the crowd, right in front of me. She saw her own black eyes looking backat her, and she was about to smile like mothers do, you know, but then saw the eyeshadow, the dress, the wilting hibiscus in my hair. "Eduardo?" she asked, her mouth looking like she was ready to suck the whole world in. God Damn I hated that name. Her forgotten plate of chicharrones slowly slipped onto the sidewalk, and I wanted to bend down and pick them up for her. I wanted to say please,

Mami. But she so shocked and I so shocked we couldn't see all the love we had right then. I ran the two blocks home in my sister's heels, and knew change was coming quick. The whole way home I saw my mami's face at that moment she recognized me—usually she see me with all the light in the world—sunk down and old, and that hit my gut like a bullet. Honey, what you can understand, running fast as hell in four-inch heels.

Everyone was yelling something. My mother, my tía, Alex screaming at them, *this is your fault, you don't discipline him, you baby him, he needs a man in his life*, and my mami yelling at him that he had no right to hit me, and me screaming, *fuck you, pendejo, you're not my father*, and *I'm sorry, Mami*, and Espie hiding in our room, her dark hair shaking around her face, packing some of my things in a duffel bag because she knew how it all be going to end. He hit me so hard in the face that I fell down as quick as the blood came, but I still spit out *you no man, you chocha, you fucking chocha*. My mother started beating on his back, *you can't hit my son, my baby, you get out of here.*

You call me a pussy? What the fuck are you, maricón? You want to know what it's like to be a woman? Do you? Let me show you, you fucking maricón. Let me fucking show you. And he grabbed my mother by the back of the throat, slammed her face against the fake wood paneling, lifted up her skirt, and fucked her. *See there, maricón?* I was screaming on the floor, blood all in my mouth, red angry and red blood, and I watched as he jerked himself in her, each time her arms flailing out to nothing but the air, a low scream like it coming from her gut, like it knew this was a death. And I watched, and I didn't move. I laid there through the whole thing, and didn't move. I couldn't move, and that's the thing. I didn't get up and beat that fucking pendejo, rip him off my mami. I just cried like a fucking spineless pansy-ass, my mami's cheek rubbed in her own spit, me whispering *sorry Mami, sorry Mami*, so low I bet she didn't hear it. I layed there after he was finished, after he fumbled with his pants, after he yelled through tears, *see maricón, see maricón*, after he left the room, after my mami slid down the wall onto the floor, her mouth still wide open but no sound coming out anymore, staring straight at me but not seeing me, both our faces laid sideways on the dirty, worn carpet.

I ran to Hollywood right away. There was no living at home after that, and it had nothing to do with me dressing all quinceñera. I wasn't a man, and clothes had shit to do with that. I knew I could never look my mami in the eye after that, couldn't see that hurt in her ever again. And knowing that took me away from mi familia, from all of it. And Hollywood was as far away as I could get from Huntington Park. That's what had to be done.

At first it was sucking guys off for a place to stay, some Craigslist hookups. I hung out at this day shelter in Hollywood called My Friend's Place, where some dipshit rich fat white girl in grad school would try to have me "write down my feelings." Shit, write down that I didn't want to be a boy anymore, that I never wanted to be a boy, but I wasn't a girl, either, and mi familia was all I knew but I couldn't be with them? Who want to read that? It was stupid, and made me feel like shit. It didn't take much time for me to find the Boulevard.

But me and Champagne, we were done with it, the hiking, the smell of cum and spit all over us and the long showers that never took it off. We'd been doing it for years, and it was time to go out before we be grannies like Mimi or Fantasia. And shit was going south, anyway, not like it be a vacay before. But it was the pinch and Mariya's OD that finally did it. We'd all been pinched before, but this time it was like a conspiracy or some shit. The fuzz came with this big-ass paddy-wagon and just scooped us *all* up, I mean really hunted us down, like rats. You should have seen the back of that van, fingernails and glitter and running mascara all over the goddamned place. And when we got there, we were too many to book. I had already wiped the lipstick off, but they didn't even throw us in, just gave us a warning, took our money, made us walk all the way back, from downtown. That was some humiliating shit, all day in the SoCal sun, burning right through my dirty-ass clothes. No one walks in L.A., and none of us gonna ride the janky-ass bus. None of us. You seen the people on that thing? Hell. The po-po knew what they were doing, and that did it for me, let me tell you.

And then Mariya, the next day, and I knew it was a sign. After she OD'd on Judas—her tongue all bit up and her eyeballs looking like they pulled out with a spoon—me and Champagne came home that night and threw all that shit away. Flush-a-lug. I knew we were chasing that shit just as much as Mariya, and I didn't want to go down that road. At first, I used to do it for kicks, but then it was something to do, keep things feeling far away when we hiking. But, hell no. Not no more. After we flushed it down, Champagne cut up some blow and promised to get serious. She was going to save the money for real now. The snip would happen. We were going to get off the Boulevard. Suck it up, do our business straight, no matter how much we hated it, get the snip, and get off the Boulevard.

"We'll do it together, just like last time," and shimmied her titties.

I watched her tilt her head back and nodding like it was the last yes there'd ever be, rubbing her nose and laughing a little in between "yes, yes." I could have been saying her wig on fire and she'd be the same way, nodding and laughing.

"Yeah, honey, that's what we'll do," I said.

She started crying, like real hard and shit, her mascara running crazy down her cheeks in big black lines.

"What is it, honey?" I asked.

She sucked the snot back in, and said to me like it was the most truthful thing she ever say to any fool, "I never wanted to be no Tutie, Lalo."

Her face was a mess, something you'd kick out of the car, let me tell you. But, there she was, and you could see the light in her even when she be fucked up as all hell. It was something like pure gold in that girl, and not that fake shit. She had the kind that shines like it coming from within, even in the dark. I reached out and wiped her face, and she rested her head in my hand.

"None of us did, honey. It's all we had." And boy, I meant that more than I thought, and it made me miss a life I hadn't even lived yet, so much.

So, I went back to the clinic where I got my titties done. His name be Dr. Alter. That the funniest goddamned thing to me, but he's good, so he be the first I thought to do the snip. Honey, 25,000 dollars just to do the deed, and then all the other bread to make that shit look real. I was like oh, Hell. It time to get serious, been fucking around long enough. I came into the efficiency that afternoon with a grin that could eat shit, and some wine and cheese—real fancy. "No more of this half-life, Champagne." I poured us a glass and we clinked and sipped it with our pinkies out. I gave her the 411 for the plan, how we'd save, how we'd get the snip within the year. One year, Champagne, we can do it. I swear the smile on that girl was enough to make you promise the world. And I told Champagne that I was for real and, honey, her eyes light up like a Christmas tree. We put our foreheads together the way we do, our fake eyelashes almost touching. We must a looked like a pair of pussy-lickers, but we didn't care.

We talked about it every night after that. We'd sit at Benito's, with our taquitos, while the other girls gone chasing the dragon.

"Real pussies?" she'd ask, like I ain't tell her a hundred times already.

"Yup, honey, one real chocha for each of us."

"They can even fuck us *in* it?"

"And it would feel good, honey. All real-like."

"Could they catch the Bug from me in my new pussy?"

"No," I lied, cuz I didn't have the heart. I had asked, cuz I knew about Champagne, but Dr. Alter said they couldn't do the snip if someone had the Bug, too hard on their bodies, low T-cell count, or some shit. I wanted to tell Champagne, but all I could do when she laid her head on my lap and waited for me to dish the story again was trace the shape of my mami's name along her arm with my fingers. No one ever talked about the Bug, but I knew most of the girls had it, cuz they were dumb bitches. I just wish Champagne hadn't been such a dumb bitch, too.

"We'll come back from the snip and start life over, just like that. Take a jimmy off, and bring a Jimmy home," I'd say, and she'd giggle into my lap. "Fall in love, get married, make dinner for our men, let them watch sports on the weekend while we go shopping. Familia."

"Nordstrom's," she would always say.

"Yes, honey, and Macy's and Saks," I'd say, and finish filing her nails.

I didn't give a shit where we go, but Champagne wanted New York City. All right, I said. It didn't make any difference to me, as long as he nice and had a nice family. As long as it wasn't on the roachy-ass Boulevard, the smell of hot piss in the afternoon. Sometimes, I'd see our dream so much I'd even forget that Champagne wasn't coming with me. But damn, how you gonna tell a girl her dream done, just like that? What she live for, then?

And Champagne was a dumb bitch. She spent way too much money on all her shit, and even though she went off Judas a la cañona, she still bought blow and Oxies. I knew she wanted the snip, and I believed she meant it, but she wasn't gonna save, not fast enough, anyway, and I definitely wasn't going to wait for her ass, I couldn't, not anymore. I know how that work, seen most of these girls never get out. And I knew she couldn't get the snip, anyway. That's why I didn't feel as bad skimming off her money stash. I'd just take the top twenty off the pile every other night, that's all. That might not seem like a lot, but that shit add up, and she never noticed, not once. Champagne was too fucked up, and I knew she couldn't see the future as clear as I did. She thought of us as some Thelma and Louise bullshit, *we'll do it together, we'll do it together*, in that baby-doll voice she had. But I didn't want to drive off no goddamned cliff. I wanted to back the hell up, punch that motherfucker into fifth gear, and roll right through to something new. I wanted to get the hell out of L.A. and meet me a nice boy who would buy me some pollo adobo at a nice restaurant and then cuddle on the couch and watch old movies together. And, after we all settled in, doing the domestic thing, that's when I'd finally go back to HP and see mi familia.

Thanksgiving. I'd get a nice dress, all nice-girl like, with flowers on it and nice sensible sandals, no heels. I'd learn to cook, and bring pibil in a casserole dish. My man would kiss my mami's hand, laugh at tia's jokes, and they'd know I'd done good for myself. I'd ask Espie about college. I know she going cuz I Google her name sometimes when I use the internets at the public library. I know she study at Cal State and her major is psychology and she in some club on campus that feed the homeless.

God damn, I couldn't wait. I also couldn't think about how it broke my heart that Champagne wouldn't be going with me. I'd just tell myself that if you think anyone is *really* with you, you a fool, plain and simple. I was going to Dr. Alter. Champagne would understand.

About a month after Champagne gone, I had my first appointment for the snip. I had 25,000. I'd been working it, more than ever, saving everything, counting it every other night. I even got a bank account, just in case Fantasia had sticky fingers. And, I was saving. I quit drinking, quit the pills, wouldn't even take them when the johnnies asked me to. I would just slip them on my tongue and spit them out when they got all into it. I needed to keep my eye on the prize. Take the money, and take the money. Snip snip, and then the new life. Take the money, milk and honey. And I did it. I did it, Champagne. Mami, I did it.

I wore the sundress that covered my knees, and took a cab to Beverly Hills. The office was in a high-rise, the marble walls so clean you could check your makeup. I felt like I was auditioning for one of the Hollywood movies, my mouth all dry and everything else sweaty. Dr. Alter met me in the waiting room and held his hand out like a gentleman, led me to his office.

"This is a very invasive surgery, Ms. Arana," he said.

"Call me, Lalo, Doctor. And you don't have to worry about that.

I been eating good, and I stop taking pills and drinking, and all that."

"That's good, Lalo. But your tests show you are HIV Positive. Did you know this? In fact, your T-cells are well below 200." He leaned towards me, the skin between his eyebrows all bunched up. "Lalo, we need to get you checked out and put on medication immediately. You need to take care of yourself."

He look like a different man, now, not a doctor but just any man, could have been a johnnie, and I was in any office. The pictures on the wall were travel posters, to Bermuda, to Paris, to The Great Wall of China, all looking fake as hell, like they were paintings, not real places. There was a clock on the wall above his head. The plants were real, one in every corner. The carpet looked like it was vacuumed right before I walked in. My hands were folded in my lap, but I couldn't feel them. I couldn't feel nothing, and something about the room got longer, like more clean carpet laid out, and I was being pulled far back from Dr. Alter. I looked down to see if I could move my hands, and they were little fists, between my legs. "I always wrap when I fuck. Every time. I'm safe."

"That's not the only way to contract the virus, Lalo. Who knows what it was. But, in your…line of work, and lifestyle, the risk is very high."

"You mean, I get the Bug from sucking dick, or something? I never heard that."

"We need to get you care right away. It's important."

I could barely ask, and I guess I knew, but needed to hear it. "No snip? Ever?"

"Your T-cell count is very low."

I walked all the way back to the efficiency. I walked along the Sunset Strip, all the rich white bitches shopping or brunching or some shit, down to Santa Monica Boulevard, the muscle queens wearing their tank tops and puffing their chest out, lattes and patio tables. And I wanted to laugh at them, how fucking stupid they looked, but I knew they had more life than me, and always would, even in their dumb-ass way. And they probably laughing at me, anyhow. How could I think I was the one tranny bitch to get up out of the Boulevard, think I was that special? That I'd have a man, have a life that looked like some straight bitch's, that I'd see mi familia again. I realized there ain't no story I heard ever end like that.

And I thought I'd been so careful, had done it as right as I could. That's the shit of it, ain't it?

Back at the efficiency I took off my dress and looked in the mirror. My titties, my long shiny hair, my flat stomach, my jimmy. My jimmy. I grabbed a trash bag and started shoving shit in there, I mean a real housecleaning. Dumped the ashtray, picked all the wrappers off the floor, even dirty stockings and clothes. If this was it, what my life was, I'd better make it clean as I could, right? At least a clean little space, clean and clear, a nice clean, fucking, tiny space. I brought the bag to Champagne's old table and swept my arm right across it—makeup, hairbands, the Wonder Woman coffee cup—all into the bag. I sat on the floor to catch my breath.

I went to the bank and took it all out, all the money I had saved for the snip. I got one of those big envelopes and put it all inside. I addressed it to Huntington Park, and wrote a note: 'I was saving this money for a real life, Mami. Go out and buy yourself one.' I stop just before I closed it up, took out the note, and added quick: 'I'm sorry.' I looked at the words, and it felt they were staring back at me, so I quickly crossed them out. I threw the note into the envelope, into the chute, and into the dark, before I could change my mind.

When I got back, I dressed up in a purple miniskirt, my red boustier, pulled my hair up with a hairband. I looked in the mirror. The tears started coming, and I slapped my own self in the face. "What you crying for, you pansy-ass bitch? You chocha. Like you got the right." They wanted to keep coming. I leaned forward, real close to the mirror, my nose almost touching. "Fuck you," I said, stared hard into my eyes for a long time, until them tears pushed all the way back, and then went out the door, to work.

About a month later, me and Cheilah be working both sides of the back alley off the

Boulevard, and an old brown El Dorado with a white replacement door drove all slow, like they do, up to me. He was in his 30s, looked like he was in good shape, and I thought maybe this one could be a little nice, for a change. When I saw his eyes, though, I could tell he was drunk as hell, and I knew he was a Carlos. Oh, well. I didn't give a fuck anymore. I'd just popped four Vicodin, so it was all smooth go for me, anyway. I was leaning into the car window. Hey, I said. Hey, he said, and unlocked the passenger door. I said something like "not even gonna compliment a girl on her outfit?" or some funny shit, and before I opened the door I heard Cheilah yelling my name all sharp and shit, she forgetting to raise it high, like we do, and hell if it ain't deep as fuck, like Barry White and some shit. The hairs on my neck came right up, cuz before I even walked across the alley and she told me, I knew what she was going to say. This was a Carlos for sure, because he was *the* Carlos. And wouldn't you fucking know, but he looked a little like my mami's old boy, Alex.

"What should we do?" Cheilah asked.

"About…?"

"I don't know, can't they fingerprint him, or do that CSI stuff on him?" Her face was real big, looking into my eyes the way she was, like she was a big moon and I was the planet she spun around. She was such a pretty girl, she really was, but it was cuz she made those eyes so round and open, and she meant them. How could she be on the Boulevard with a sweet face like that? Like Champagne. I wanted to cup that face in my hand, and kiss it. And then slap the shit out of it.

I dropped my own face, instead, away from her sight. I let the hair fall all around it. "No, honey, they wouldn't do nothing."

"Then, what we gonna do?" She was wringing her hands then.

I looked back at the car. Champagne died in that car.

"What we gonna do, Lalo?"

A fucking El Dorado. That just be the shit of it, no, to not just die in a Carlos' car, but in that piece of shit. That piece of shit.

"Lalo, what we gonna do?"

I grabbed her wrists hard—even surprised myself—but I was shaking, like the question was some kind of attack on me. I looked her in the eyes like a tiger, and I wanted to hug her and tell her why, but what that gonna do if you haven't figured it out for yourself? I wasn't gonna kill her dream cuz mine done. I wasn't gonna bullshit her, either.

"What we gonna *do*? We gonna go to *work*, honey."

I dropped her arms and turned back towards the El Dorado.

"Lalo!" Now, this was said with all the high pitch, and then some. My name was shrieked at me, like a dog caught pissing on the floor, or a child about to put her finger in a light socket. Cheilah was fire red, balling her fists, tears coming down her face. "No."

It took everything I got, and I even breathed in some before I said it, cuz I knew it killed me, too. "It's what we do, honey," and kept myself together, like a statue. One stone cold bitch, because that what it take.

And she spit on me. Chucked one up right at my face. Got me clean on the cheek and eyelid. "Puta," she said, "you fucking puta," and walked away.

I watched her stomp around the corner, wiped the spit away. It's fine if she want to be like that. I knew why. She was young, still thought there was something else after this, an after this, at all. She'll learn that being all high and mighty and all Kumbaya don't mean shit. Her friends will die, she'll get the Bug. Shit, her dreams dead by the time she first walk the Boulevard, and there ain't nothing more. At least I'd get her ready for the rest of it.

Carlos was too fucked to know what was going on with me and Cheilah. Inside the car, I saw that he had already taken his jacket off. I rubbed him through his jeans to get him started, and asked him what he wanted to do. He didn't say nothing, buried his face, kissed me on the neck. "Oh, honey, that's good," I said, and I wanted to stick my nails in his skull. "What you want Lalo to do for you?"

He hiked my skirt up real fast and started stroking me. "Is that what you want, honey?" I asked, and he whimpered, then reached into the back seat and grabbed a condom, tore open the package, and slid it down my jimmy. I said, "sure, honey."

See, Champagne said no to Carlos, and that's why she dead. I looked down at my jimmy. And honey, that's why he dead. "Sure, honey."

He was young for a Carlos, and kind of had a sweet face. I tried to imagine him angry, enough to hurt Champagne the way he did. He probably was a nice motherfucker before his dreams taken away, too. Isn't that what it all is, why we all get so nasty? My teeth grit a lot more, now, I tell you that.

I did him from behind, how he wanted it. Still only whimpering, he held onto the dashboard, pushing himself back at me. As I got faster, his voice got higher. "You like me fucking you, baby?" I asked him, but he was gone, gone far away, into that place we all go when we dead. He didn't hear me, didn't see the streetlight glaring into the window, and didn't feel the temperature do that drop it does when the night wears on in L.A. I bet he was flying, way past his whole life, honey, somewhere beyond the cigarette-burned insides of his El Dorado, past the wife that was waiting for him back home, past the city limits, if there were any. Maybe he was even flying past Champagne's busted up body, her tittie popped out of the halter top, arms bent into the concrete like she was dancing to her favorite song, her bruises the color of an L.A. sunset when it hasn't rained for months.

I kept at it, and looked outside the car window, too, could see a little bit of Benito's behind the warehouse, the counter where we'd play the game. Champagne ask, leaning against the counter all sweet, "Where'd you be right now if not here? Tell me, Lalo."

I sighed, like one do. Oh, Champagne. I'd be doing something besides fucking this whimpering Carlos in the back of a jank-ass car, the smell of his shit and sweat on my hands, on my tongue, and Champagne's face staring back at me from that little corner of Benito's. *We'll do it together. We'll do it together.* Her face in my hands, her laughing at some funny shit I said, her looking at me sometimes like I was the last bitch in the world who told the truth. Those times when we were woot-wooted in the Yukon Diner because we believed we were that fucking hot, when we danced at the club to get the Boulevard out of our heads, eating our Del Taco and picturing the men we'd meet when we done got the snip, thinking this all was the means to some end, and not the end from the beginning.

And her busted up dead body in the concrete, her mouth wide open but no sound coming out anymore, staring straight at me but not seeing me.

I moved my hand from Carlos' cock to my own, but I kept pumping. I wrapped my fingers around me, and rolled the rubber off, but I kept pumping, and dropped it to the floor. Carlos kept whimpering. And I kept pumping, and thought about the handsome boy who was never going to carry me up the stairs, that I would never curl up with on a couch, who'd never meet mi familia. Mi familia. And when I came inside Carlos, I bit my lip, didn't make a sound, but made sure that I was all the way up in there. I filled him up, filled him up with everything I was and everything I was never gonna be, motherfucker, and kept going after that, just to make sure. I leaned down to his ear, and said real softly through my gritted teeth, so he didn't know I be crying, "you want to know what it's like to be a woman? Do you? Do you, Carlos?" and I kept going after that, because what else is there.

EYE WALL

Zelia Huberty isn't Omarr's first crush, but it feels different than the ones he's had this year on Angela Morales and Yesenia Roberts. This one makes his limbs feel hot, a searing heat, as if his body is a house and the whole thing is on fire. The other two girls elicited chills through his belly, clammy hands he worried would have them think he was a piece of uncooked chicken if he touched them. In Zelia's case, he's afraid he'll burn her. She is in the grade above him, but they share chorus and lunch period. That's where he saw her, in chorus. She was new, smiling shyly while stumbling for her seat among the altos, close to him in the tenor section. He could see her, watch her without awkwardness, since she was on the same bench level as he was. She had dark hair, like most of the girls in the school, but her skin was remarkably pale and smooth, like cream squeezed from an éclair. He found it so beautiful, and predicted that her thoughts and voice would be just as smooth as the pearly skin that encased them.

He saw her again in his neighborhood, on his way to his mother's favorite panadería. Zelia was getting into a small blue car with what looked to be her parents and little sister. She lived in his neighborhood.

That made it even more special. She was local, they could meet halfway between their houses and ride bikes to the park. It was perfect.

And now he watches her during lunch period, this new girl in school, two tables over, watches her first open her milk carton and drink it all, then eat all of the corn before taking a bite of the pizza square, and then lastly eating the fruit cocktail, bright red half cherry the final bite. He watches her listen to Abby Rodriguez with a tilt to her head. Omarr adores this lopsided pose, like caring mothers do in the movies, is convinced it is because she wholeheartedly wants to listen to Abby's story, that she is the sort of girl who cares about her friends. The kind of girl who wants to be a teacher, or a nurse.

Even though he's sitting with his two best friends, Josh and David, and knows they will make fun of him once they realize he's walked over to a girl in the cafeteria, once they see him tap the light purple t-shirted shoulder of Zelia, and she turns her neck and gives him a small polite smile, and waits with her large brown eyes, and he asks her if she would like to go ride bikes after school today, and is surprised at how fast she says "sure" with a light shrug of her shoulders that also says *why not?* and he says "cool" and "see ya later," and he walks back to his table without moving his head and arms, which inspires some of the others at Zelia's table to giggle behind him, and he sits back down in front of his lunch knowing that he won't be able to eat another bite, knowing that his face is definitely, most certainly, red, even beneath his sun-deepened yet already brown skin, and Josh and David will see how pink he's flushed, and how ready they are with their "oooohhh"s and rapid-fire songs of half-rhyming ridicule (*Omarr and Zelia, sittin' in a tree...*), and he knows it will embarrass him, with a feeling so similar to pain, one that he gets with too much attention thrust on him, he does it anyway.

And when the bell rings for next period, Omarr knows he only has three periods to go, math, PE and social studies, before the final bell will release him, and he gets picked up by his big sister in front of the school, and once home he jumps on his bike and meets Zelia exactly at the corner between their two houses.

*

James is called in to the tiny windowless room on the first level of the parking garage that functions as the office for the small security firm that hired him to guard a construction site, a five-story condo building. The building looks like any other in San Ysidro, stucco, boxy and the color of the land on both sides of the border—parched is the word that comes to James' mind, for all of San Ysidro. The air, the land, the people.

His boss must be twenty-five, a good fifteen years younger than James, another sucker who probably thought he was making something of himself by sticking with the security firm since graduating high school. This guy is a dime a dozen, James can tell. He wants to give the kid some advice, the simple logic that one can't go places if they don't move.

James is getting fired. His boss begins with questions, like how do you like the firm, and do you feel you've been treated fairly here. James knows how this ends, when the boss asks you those types of questions. He's been down this road before, the welding company, the mortuary.

"Some of your co-workers feel a bit uncomfortable working with you," his boss says.

Sammy. It's Sammy. The young kid who dropped out of community college and took the security job because he got his girlfriend pregnant. James often caught Sammy staring at his right arm with a face of fear or disgust, the involuntary twitching it makes since the motorcycle accident.

"They complain that you freak them out with some of the things you say," his boss says.

You mean the truth, James thinks. About what's going on in this country, about how society is buckling under its own weight. About the economic collapse that will happen any day now. How international bankers are manipulating the Federal Reserve, and fucking over Americans. How the middle class is being squeezed, so slowly and steadily that they don't even realize their head will explode any moment. How Soviet aggression is everywhere. If that freaks these kids out, then they are even more in the dark than he thought. These kids know nothing. He is surrounded by idiots worrying about where they're going out on Friday night and getting their next piece of ass, about prime time soap opera storylines, who shot who, and who has amnesia, and who wears it best, and "maybe it's Maybelline."

"It's more the way you talk about these things," his boss says.

"How should I talk?" James asks. He wants to add *when no one is listening.*

James is getting fired. The Hubertys just moved here, he and his wife, Etna, and their two daughters, Cassandra and Zelia. They just moved into their apartment, and now he is unemployed again. And ever since the motorcycle accident it's been harder and harder to find a job. He can't weld anymore, and he did that for so long there wasn't any other skill he cultivated. This is exactly the problem, what he's been telling his co-workers while they stand around and do nothing but watch the construction crew throw up cookie-cutter condos that will cost too much for any of them to buy, anyway.

James wants to hurt his boss, his now former boss, not because he is particularly bad, but because he is clueless, unaware that he feeds into the bullshit, furthers the slow disintegration of the working class, the middle class, the true American people, the ones who built this country, and the very same people who are fucking so blind they can't see how the system is fucking them, stupid feeble sheep who let their murderers lead them to the slaughter. Pathetic, stupid people. He wants to hurt his boss, wants to grab him by the neck and lift him high, watch the air leave his body while his limbs dance erratically, all because of James' hand. It would be one less sheep, one less meaningless idiot in an already too populated country.

James points a trembling finger at his boss, his fury channeled into this one single gesture. He says nothing. And then turns and limps out of the white cinderblock office and into the hot California summer afternoon.

*

Omarr and Zelia are riding bikes again. This time, they zip along Averil Road to Blackshaw Lane, where there are fewer cars to worry about. They weave through parallel-parked minivans, small apartment buildings, palm trees. Blackshaw is a nicer street, with single-family houses, large yards, and fruit trees. Omarr lives on this street. He rides behind Zelia, because he likes watching her hair flow away from her face; he thinks it's really pretty. She looks back occasionally, and smiles, the sunlight forcing her eyes to squint. Omarr thinks it looks like a wink, like they have a secret between them. He hopes they will tell secrets to each other, maybe even make a secret. He would love to share a secret with her, that only the two of them know.

One of the yards is full of people, his neighbors celebrating a quinceñera. He can see the girl dressed up in a big white dress, eating carnitas and tortillas. Lola Beltran emanates from somewhere in the house. He wonders if Zelia has ever had carnitas. She told him that there weren't many Mexicans in Ohio, where she moved from. He wants to introduce her to his favorite foods: adovada, birria and, of course, his mami's pozole. He sees the mariachi band setting up and yells to Zelia and points. "Look," he says.

She sees the men decked out in their Charros and red string ties. "That's so cool!"

Omarr loves that Zelia is impressed with his culture, that she asks him to teach her Spanish words. He has taught her some naughty ones, and how to order at the heladeria down the street, since the owners don't speak English.

Zelia peels off her bike and runs up to an orange tree. "I didn't know oranges grew like this!" She positions herself under one fully fruited, and looks to Omarr. "Can I?"

He nods, "Duh. That's what they're there for." He smiles, and pulls it off the tree.

After she peels the orange, she tears it neatly, and hands him the larger half. They sit on the curb and let the juice dribble off their hands and chins. "I think I'm going to like it here," she says. Her fingers are yellow around the nails, her lips wet from the juice. Omarr's whole body warms up. He really likes Zelia Huberty.

*

James and Etna are sitting in the living room, watching TV. The girls are in their room doing homework. Etna has already noticed James' twitching, more than usual, his fingers fisting, then splaying, fisting then splaying. She's nervous this might be the beginnings of a fight, but she doesn't know what it would be about. She's knows he lost his job, but she hasn't said anything about that, knows not to nag him or share her worries, wants to ride it out. Besides, James will get a new job. He always does.

"Babe, I got a problem," he says, still staring at the TV.

Her body tenses, but she slides her hand onto his. "You're OK."

"No."

"It's just a bit of bad luck. There's all kinds of jobs out here."

"That's not it." He looks at her for the first time. "Of course I'll get a job. I've always provided for this family."

Etna's hairs on her neck rise up. "I know, Jimmy. I know. That's what I'm saying."

"So, you don't have to say it."

"You're right, Jimmy," she says, and rubs the top of his hand.

They are silent for a minute. Etna has forgotten what TV program they're watching. Something with bright colors and a laugh track. Something familiar, but she can't seem to connect what she sees with what she knows.

"It's different, Etna. My mind is all mixed up," James says.

"How so?"

"Some of my thoughts. Like, thoughts I've had before, like in passing, but that I could push away. Now, they stay there."

"What you mean, Jimmy?"

James turns to her. "You ever get on the edge of a building, or a cliff, something high up with an edge, and you feel this urge to jump? Not because you actually want to die or nothing. Have you ever felt that pull?"

Etna doesn't respond, not sure what would be the right thing to say. She waits.

"Lately, I've been having thoughts like that, only I linger on them longer, like if I was on that edge I would jump."

Etna tilts her head. "Jimmy, you want to kill yourself?"

James sighs. "No, Etna, that thought of jumping was an example."

"Well, what then?"

James looks up at the ceiling, moves his lips around like there's something in his mouth he needs to rearrange, like his words are marbles that he's summoning from under his tongue.

"I have…thoughts. Of hurting people."

Etna furrows her brow, looks into his face, which has taken on a vulnerability, everything open like a child's. Somehow saying the words aloud releases a feeling in James. Like if he said it more, the more the feelings would leave.

Etna laughs.

She says, "Well, of course you want to hurt people. I want to hurt people every day. Just wring their necks. That's normal, Jimmy. People are assholes."

And just as quick as James' face opened up, it clouded over, the darkness quite visible, especially around the eyes and mouth.

Etna sees this quick change, and that is when she realizes she doesn't understand, after all, and that scares her. She is afraid to ask anything more, because she doesn't recognize this face of her husband's, not quite, even though they've been together almost twenty years. And they have had their share of fights, have come to blows before, have hurt each other. She once even called the cops to report that James messed up her jaw bad enough to need medical attention. She knew James had a temper. Hell, so did she. But this look was different, just a bit, even in the dark room she could tell it was something else. But she was afraid to figure out what it was. She needed to say something, though.

"Why don't you talk to someone about it. You know, a professional, one of those free clinics," she says.

James' face brightens a bit. "Yeah, that's a good idea."

Etna smiles. She is happy to have said the right thing. Sometimes, that's all one can do.

"Come on," she says. I'll read your Tarot." She grabs his hand, leads him to their room. As she closes the door, she hears her daughters talking softly in their shared bedroom, probably something about boys, or school. Their voices make her feel calm, that everything will be all right. The world is moving as it should.

*

When he doesn't see Josh and David out front of the school before first bell, where they always wait for each other, Omarr knows that something is up, but he doesn't think it has to do with him. That is, until he opens his locker and sees the picture. It is sloppy, outlined in black marker, but clear in what it depicts: a boy, shaded in brown marker, and a girl, signified with six long black lines coming from her head and arced along both her sides, three lines each. She also has little sideways commas, to suggest her small, barely-there boobs. And, in particularly crude dimension, an absurdly large wiener and balls jut from the boy's stick legs. The wiener doesn't disappear into the girl—looks more like it rests on her belly with this rendering—but Omarr knows that is the suggestion. And from the tip of the wiener are five little lines. The girl has an O for a mouth and two little black dots for eyes.

Omarr is furious. He shouldn't have told Josh and David that Zelia invited him over for family dinner. Omarr saw the beginnings of their sneers then. He stomps into homeroom with no concern that he will get in trouble. He is angry at his friends' disrespect. It is one thing to draw his wiener on Zelia, but that's not what upsets him most. It is the look on her face, the dots and the O, like she is a doll, or a puppet, something that makes her less than what she is. And that is what makes him so furious. Furious enough to walk right up to Josh, because he knows that Josh drew it even if the both conceived of it together, and before he can even see Josh's smirk, his acknowledgement of the prank, Omarr pushes him hard, so hard that the desk chair combo that Josh half-sits, half-stands in falls backward with Josh, surprised, flailing his arms to catch something. Luckily, another student's backpack softens his fall, and fellow students quickly assist Josh, or look at Omarr with a mouth remarkably similar to Josh's crude drawing of Zelia's, an almost perfect and somehow vulgar O.

Omarr feels the hands of his homeroom teacher on his shoulders, and is sent to the principal's office. He is not yet worried about being in trouble, or his punishment. He is upset, yes, his body still hot and shaky, but is oddly satisfied, that his hands on Josh equaled the power of the drawing in some way, that he canceled out the transgression, and they were even. He doesn't let go of this satisfaction, even as he is suspended for the rest of the day, and sent home. Omarr thinks that maybe this is what justice feels like, no longer a word solely in a history textbook or a comic book, but a real feeling, one that he is able to conjure, one in which he is able to participate.

*

James sits down at the edge of the sofa and dials the number Etna found in the phonebook, of the mental health hotline, that she gave him before heading to work. He dials the number slowly, aware that he doesn't know what to expect from this call, but that he needs to speak to someone about these escalating urges. The woman on the other line has a thin voice, a little breathy, could almost be a Midwestern accent, maybe a little Ohio in there? She first asks him if there is immediate risk to his own life. He assumes she means suicide, to which he replies, "no."

"Is this an emergency?" she asks.

James doesn't know how to answer this, exactly. He indeed is scared by how quickly the urges he feels have become more and more compelling since he was fired from the security firm, how the knowledge he already affirms repeatedly—about the international banking system, about Communist infiltration, about the demise of the working class—sharpens itself from blunt subjects of ire into piercing demands that make him want to hurt, to exact pain, not on anything in particular, but on everything in particular. But when he thinks of emergency, he imagines someone who is weak, someone who needs in spite of their abilities. That's not him. He is a fighter. He is a man who has worked to provide for his family, despite all obstacles. And, he is a man who keeps his eyes open to the injustices in the world, all while the people around him stay blind—no, choose to blind themselves—to the truth. He is a soldier in this war, to wake people up. He is a warrior, a lone vigilante, to fight against complacency, to rid the country of ignorance. It's urgent, but he's not a victim here. He will never be a victim, because he is a fighter. Kill or be killed.

He says, "It's not an emergency."

"What is the nature of your call, sir?"

James searches for the words, and says, "I'm having thoughts. Really awful thoughts, about people."

She asks for his name. He shares it, along with his contact information. And then she says they will call him right back, and to "hang in there." That she was glad he called.

And he knows more than ever that he needs to speak with someone. Simply sharing the little he did with this woman broke open the need even more. He thought he described it to Etna perfectly, that feeling one gets when they peer over a ledge, a precipice, and have that overwhelming desire to jump. For what? Not to end a life, or to know what it feels like, but because we *can*. That's what it's about. And the urges he feels lately flood him so completely that he thinks he could perform them. It's no longer the common fantasy of pulling someone out of their driver-side window when they cut him off. It's no longer imagining him whip his gun out and point right at his boss' skull—his former boss—and watching the pipsqueak wet his pants in fear. He wants to pull that trigger, really pull it. And then pull it again, have the bullets spray forth from his gun, but really the bullets spraying forth from him, the one who holds the gun, the one who controls the gun. The control.

He sits and waits for the mental health center to call him back.

Little does he know, the receptionist with the thin, breathy voice does not assign his case an immediate call back. James informed her that he was not a threat to himself (a 5 Alert), and that his call was not an emergency (a 4 Alert). And the receptionist heard nothing unsettling in James' voice, nothing that would have her think a he was a 3 Alert, based on the training she received. She was trained to listen for certain triggers, words, tones, voice cadences. This man was at best a 2 Alert. 5, 4 and 3 Alert calls need to be attended to first. And the center gets so many calls. It's not that they want to prioritize the calls, but they have limited resources, limited time. They have to filter through the hundreds of calls they get daily, and do what they can to help those most in need. She fills out the brief form and drops it into the 2 Alert stack on her desk. Most likely, they will get to James' call in three days—that is their average—when they are fully staffed and it's not close to a major holiday, like New Years. Most likely, this man will hang in there, and once the center addresses the 3, 4, and 5 Alerts, they can help this man, who is having really awful thoughts, about people.

And, even if the center did get around to following up with the stack of 2 Alerts—which they don't—they wouldn't be able to specifically call James. The receptionist jotted his name down as Shouberty, and reversed two of the numbers in his home telephone.

*

The shame is fully realized once home, when Adelina, Omarr's mother, unleases a litany of worries and disappointments. Suspended? Her boy? What made him do such a thing? Who taught him to hit a boy, and in school? And while Omarr tries to insist that he didn't hit Josh, that he merely pushed him, and that Josh isn't even hurt, his mother wants nothing of these details, with a curt gesture of her palm similar to swearing under oath. Her son was suspended, and that is what hurts her. In her string of words she convinces herself that she must have done something wrong, that she failed to recognize this wicked potential in him. "We didn't come all the way from Mexico for you to become this kind of boy." This is when Omarr forgets all about the justice he felt for defending his girl's honor. *His girl.* Hours ago, it felt like the right thing to do. But seeing his mother holding back tears, rattling through the kitchen, picking up a pot, then dropping it absently on the counter, opening the fridge and selecting nothing, looking back at him, the satisfaction that surged through him dissolves just as quickly, like a final scene in a movie. Looking at him. He only wants to wave his hands in the space between them and what it is, to wave it away. His own face swells with the promise of crying.

"It's those boys, mijo. Those boys you play with. They aren't good boys. I've told you that."

And this is true. She has warned him about Josh and David, about them throwing bottles in empty parking lots just to watch them shatter on the pavement, about the way they treat their little sisters, about the cursing. And it's true, Josh and David do curse, and David talks back to his mother in a way that Omarr's father would never allow, or that Omarr would ever try.

But they are his friends. They live in the neighborhood. They ride bikes with him, and they play Atari at David's house, and they have fun.

But Omarr is also mad at David and Josh, for the drawing, something he would never do, and what his mother says makes sense now. What kind of boys do these things?

"You keep hanging out with them, and who knows what they'll pressure you to do. That's how it starts, mijo. You become the people you associate with."

This seems to calm his mother down, saying this one thing, like she tried out all her other words to find this important truth. And once she says it, she sits down at the kitchen table across from him, and this time not with anger or disappointment, but with her usual tenderness. Omarr can't help but hear this. A couple memories flood into him, moments where he did do things he wasn't proud of with Josh and David. He's thrown a bottle. He's said curse words, of course only around them. He knows his mother is right.

He decides right then that he can't be friends with Josh and David, anymore. He needs to associate himself with people that do the right thing, that don't curse and break things and draw nasty pictures and tack them on his locker. He needs to hang around the good people, so that he can be a good person. He needs to hang around Zelia.

And like his mother knows he has made this choice right then, she reaches over to him, runs her hands through his hair and pulls their faces together, kisses his forehead, and wraps her arms tight around his shoulders.

*

James rides his motorcycle along San Ysidro Boulevard. The cool night air, the speed of the bike, the closeness he feels to the street. This, he is in control of; it soothes him, pushes the awful thoughts to somewhere farther back in his mind. They are there, but they are muted by the wind, the focus of the bike. He wishes he could keep riding, circle around his neighborhood until the thoughts disappear completely. He knows they won't do that, however, that they never go away entirely, even when he rides. At least they aren't in the front of his mind, though, like they are when he's alone in the house, surrounding him, like a swarm of summer gnats, always catching up to him when he's still.

He waited for the call back from the mental health center for hours, didn't leave the sofa, afraid to leave the spot, what might happen if he did, the fever roiling, growing in his head, as if any sudden movement on his part would trigger something, something explosive. The jump. Then, Etna came home from work. When she walked in the door, she immediately sensed his anguish, he could tell. He wanted so badly for the center to call him, to tell him how to make the thoughts stop, and the fever in his head to subside, so he could step away from the edge.

Etna hesitated to greet him, lingered at the front door, her hand on the knob. He didn't know what he must have looked like right then, the thoughts so powerful that he was afraid to move.

"Jimmy?"

"I'm still waiting."

She nodded, her hand circling the doorknob.

"Are the girls in their room?"

He had forgotten about the girls. He must have seen them come home from school, but he couldn't remember.

Etna called their names, and James assumed they peeked their heads in the hallway, because he saw Etna nod towards their bedroom door.

She took a few steps toward him. "Jimmy. Zelia is having a friend over for dinner, remember? She and Cassie are making shepherd's pie for him. Omarr, from around the corner. Remember?"

He didn't remember. How could he, with all this pressure in his head, the fever?

"They're making friends," Etna said, with a forced smile.

The thought of his daughters making shepherd's pie together in the small kitchen was nice. Etna made it for special occasions, her family's recipe. And his daughters. The only good thing he'd ever done. Zelia and Cassandra.

"I'm gonna go for a ride, just to..."

"Okay, that sounds good."

"Okay."

And it is a good idea, a better idea, than sitting on the sofa waiting for other people to try and help him. He should know by now that never happens, anyway, there's no one to help him, there never was. There was only his family. Everyone else was clueless, ignorant to what the country was doing to them. They went along with it, pretending they didn't see the festering rot of it all, just watching TV and eating, and eating, and eating, like pigs.

James rounds the intersection of San Ysidro again, perhaps for the twentieth time, concentrates on the road, feels the wind on his chest, cooling the fever. Just a few more laps, and he'll head home.

*

Omarr dresses up for dinner. His mother advised him to wear one of his church outfits, the navy chinos and white button-up with small blue sailboats. He foregoes the bowtie, thinks it's too church, too dorky.

The Huberty's apartment is small, with lots of stuff on the walls. Pictures of the family, Zelia and her little sister, other people he imagines are family back in Ohio. Zelia's mother collects small spoons from different places around the country, and hangs them in a diagonal pattern between the windows in the living room. And there are shelves everywhere, in every room, with canned fruits and vegetables, Spam, rolls of toilet paper, flashlights, batteries. Zelia tells him it's all her father's. "To prepare for a Communist invasion. We used to have a basement that was like a bunker. We could live in it, in case of a nuclear attack."

And then there are the guns. All kinds of them. The small ones that police officers shoot with, but also the machine guns Omarr sees soldiers carrying in war movies, and really long rifles, all along the hallway. "There's some in Dad's bedroom, too." Omarr has never seen anything like it, and stares at them like they are displayed treasures. But they also make him nervous. He wonders what Mr. Huberty is like. Like a military commander? A vigilante? One of those guys who can live alone in the woods with just a knife and flint? The photo on the wall doesn't look anything like those guys, and more like Mr. Daldry, his fifth grade science teacher—balding head, skinny neck, glasses, nerdy smile. But the guns and the ammo and the canned food convinces Omarr that he needs to make a good impression on Mr. Huberty. He needs to prove to him that he associates with the right people, that he is one of the good kids, that he is good for Zelia.

And just as he makes this decision, just as Zelia and Cassandra and their mother sit down at the table, and Zelia drops a heaping spoon of some kind of mashed potatoes mixed with beef and other stuff on his plate, the front door opens, and Mr. Huberty walks in, wearing a black motorcycle jacket, helmet under his arm. He kisses Zelia's mother, then the girls.

"You must be Zelia's friend," he says.

Omarr half stands in his chair, shakes Mr. Huberty's offered hand. "Yes, sir."

Their eyes meet for a moment. Omarr can't quite read them. They are really calm. He is really calm. He is smiling and shaking Omarr's hand, but Omarr doesn't feel any warmth looking at him, like he's not really a person and more like a clone, or a robot, like a fake version of a real Mr. Huberty. He is reminded for a second time of Mr. Daldry, but this time a lesson from his class, when they discussed hurricanes. Mr. Daldry said that the most intense part of a hurricane, with the most furious winds, occurs at the eye wall, near the center. But the dead center of the hurricane, the eye itself, is absolutely still. Mr. Daldry described it as eerie, no sounds, not even bugs or birds, the calmest, quietest thing you'll ever see.

Omarr feels he needs to make the best impression on this father for he and Zelia to remain friends. With all these guns, he never wants to see Mr. Huberty's eye wall.

*

When he wakes up the fever is strong, already pulling him to the jump before he's risen out of bed. It is almost dizzying for the thoughts to enter him so early, to press around his head so immediately. He thinks of the call that he never got, how he was forgotten, how he is forgotten often, and the fever increases, and a phrase keeps playing across his mind, like a banner advertisement: *Society had their chance. Society had their chance.*

James suggests the family go to the San Diego zoo. He can't ride his motorcycle all day. And, the only other thing he can think will make him feel better is spending time with his daughters. Sure, they have no money, and he still doesn't have a job lined up, but right now controlling the thoughts is more important than the family bank account. A beautiful day out with his beautiful girls. Maybe this will help. He needs the relief.

The zoo is full of families. It is one of those perfect San Diego summer days, a clear blue sky, faint traces of blooming plumeria carried along the soft breeze. Etna and James stroll behind the girls, who zig-zag to each exhibit. Etna is quiet, a little tense. He can tell by the way her hand sweats when she touches him. It makes him feel more uneasy, and he thinks about the word disease—dis-ease—and fully understands the word, now. That word is so often used, tossed into sentences, and no one really thinks about what it truly means. And that is what he really feels, a dis-ease, a disease.

He asks the girls what they are looking at, to break him out of the loop of his thoughts. "A caracal," Cassandra yells back. "It's a like a cat with big ears."

"Oh yeah. Where's it from?"

James continues this type of interruption whenever the edge gets close, when the fever builds, the swarming of gnats. "What are you looking at now?" It helps, even if just a little. With all these people looking at the animals, their stupid, clueless faces gawking at marsupials, pointing at them, not reading the information about them, not learning, just gawking. Like the exhibit is a fucking TV show, and not a connection to the science of our planet. And these people have jobs, better jobs than he has, because they do whatever it takes. They laugh at their boss' stupid jokes, they agree with everything their bosses say, they lick their boss' ass, they fuck their boss in the storeroom, just to keep the job they don't even care about. And because he has an opinion, and because he shares it, he is fired. He is ridiculed, seen as inappropriate, seen as creepy. All these people in the zoo, all drinking the Kool-Aid. And they point and laugh at the animals, make stupid noises. They don't even read the information the zoo provides.

"What are you looking at now?"

"A dhole. It looks like a fox."

He sees all these people, not in their t-shirts and flip-flops here in the zoo, but at work, in their button-up shirts and ties, in their wedges and knee-length skirts, in their brass-buckled belts, clomping around sterile offices and retail outlets, laughing at jokes that aren't funny, faces ha ha ha-ing with high-pitched fake mouths, fake hair, fake nails, fake tits, fake faces. They don't even know what they do. They don't make anything. Where are the true American workers, the ones that built this country? Why did the country snuff those that made this country what it is, that purpose, to make things for others? Now it's all how can I get the promotion for a job I don't like? What do I need to do? For me, for me, for me.

"What are you looking at now?"

"Hamadryas baboon. From Saudi Arabia and Somalia."

James goes up to the exhibit this time, to look at something else, to redirect his attention, to learn about Hamadryas baboons. There's a couple dozen, all actively running around, rolling over each other, smacking their lips at each other. The ones with the large manes around their necks, the males—that these idiots would know if they read the fucking information cards!—act aggressively. He's not sure why, but they show their teeth, even bite the legs of the smaller baboons, the females, if they wander away from him. This gets some of the other males riled up, and they make a screeching sounds, and run around the enclosure. Then, the largest male runs up the raucous, perches on a high stone, while the others screech at each other, swiping the dirt like they're looking for something they've dropped. The screeches get louder, and in a sudden move, the large alpha male jumps into the fray and mounts one of the screeching males from behind. James is too stunned to think about his daughters, who are giggling next to him. The alpha male pumps away while the other males are zipping around the spectacle, screeching so loud that it hurts James' ears. But he can't stop looking, because he recognizes something in these baboons, in their scurrying, in their nonsensical screaming and screeching, how they allow this one baboon to control them, how they scramble in his presence, how they dig for him, how they let him fuck them in the ass. The fever fills him, the edge pulls close, and fury burns his eye sockets. James isn't angry at the alpha. He's angry at all those other fucking baboons that take it, that run around ignorant to their weakness, those stupid animals letting this one control them, supplicating themselves. The weakness disgusts him. The weakness. It needs to end.

Etna walks up to James, who is now blankly staring at the screeching throng. She places her hand on his back. "Those things are crazy." She chuckles.

James maintains his gaze on the Hamadryas baboons. His mouth is dry. He understands now that he must sacrifice himself for something greater, that in order to address how fucked up the country has become, he must allow the fever, to stop fighting it. He needs to walk up to the edge, and not fight the urge to jump. This is what he needs to do.

Still facing the baboon enclosure, their lip-smacking and dirt-digging, their screeching and scampering, James knows he has to stop fighting, but he's afraid, afraid of what that will lead to, that future. He knows it won't be long for him, once he jumps. But he's afraid. He needs to make the first step, to commit to the edge. Something that will assure he follows through, a vow of sorts, that will have him cross over from resistance to allowance of his fate. *Society had their chance.* So, it is to his wife, Etna, that he professes the vow that will now take him to the edge, that will have him embrace the fever, and jump, with no turning back.

He says, "My life is effectively over."

*

Omarr is riding his bike around the neighborhood, alone. Yards are a flurry of activity with afternoon barbeques and Tejano music, and Omarr sails through the different smells, the various meats on the grill. Zelia was at the zoo with her family, and he is no longer associating with Josh and David, so there is no one to play with. All of the laughter and music in the yards on both sides makes him feel even more lonesome.

And just as he resolves to go back home and perhaps help his mother around the house, or watch TV, he sees Josh and David, rounding the corner. They wave at him. Omarr thinks to pretend he didn't see it, and continue on. They approach him on their own bikes, and Omarr freezes. He realizes that while he had repeated over and over to himself that he wouldn't hang out with Josh and David anymore, he didn't devise a plan for what he'd say to them if he saw them. How stupid! When! Of course he'd see them! And he didn't think about what this moment would look like, what he would say. And now, they approach.

"Hey," David says.

"Hey," Omarr replies, and looks down at his shoes.

David gives Josh a *go ahead, do it!* look.

Josh sighs. "Listen, man. I'm sorry about the drawing."

Omarr keeps his head down.

"For real. Okay?"

Omarr nods. "Okay."

"Cool."

David says, "We're gonna go to McDonald's. My mom gave me some money. Come on."

He knows he shouldn't associate with these boys, that he needs to make his mother proud, that he needs to make a good impression on Mr. Huberty, so that he can be friends with good people the right people, like Zelia.

"No, that's OK. I'm gonna go home, help my mom."

David says, "Oh, come on, Omarr. No hard feelings. I'll get you a milkshake."

And now Omarr is torn. Josh did apologize, and that is the quality of a good person, and maybe they weren't so bad after all. And it will suck if he doesn't have any friends in the neighborhood, especially when Zelia's busy doing stuff with her family, like today. Maybe he can still be friends with Josh and David, but he'll spend less time with them. He won't go to empty parking lots and throw bottles against the asphalt, he'll leave Josh's house when they finish playing video games and out of boredom start prank calling the ugly girls in their school. He'll limit his interactions, so that he can still spend more time with the right people, but won't be lonely.

And what's one visit to McDonald's?

*

Once they get home from the zoo, Cassandra and Zelia immediately go to their room, and Etna says she's tired and wants to lie down for a minute. James watches his family disappear into the cavities of the apartment.

He knows what he needs to do, and decides not to hesitate. Nothing can slow down a man who has gone to the familiar edge and has finally made the jump. He goes into the closet and pulls out a red checkered blanket, unfolds it and lays it on the table. He then grabs his 9mm Browning, his 12-gauge Winchester, the 9mm Uzi carbine, and all the ammo he has for them. Three very different guns for different kinds of war. There are many wars within one man, and it's best to prepare for them all.

As he fills the blanket, the resolve he felt at the zoo is fortified. The fever has subsided, almost as if this decision is the aspiration coursing through him, that sense of relief. He knows now the fever was his resistance to his fate, not a disease. He is not the disease. The baboons are the disease. And diseases must be cured. And sometimes, that requires sacrifice.

He peers into his daughters' bedroom. They look up from their books. He doesn't want to prolong this, because if anything it will make him hesitate. And he can't hesitate. He has already jumped.

"Goodbye. I won't be back," he says.

He walks into his bedroom. He has to be quick. Etna is half-awake. He is not going to kiss her, or say anything like a farewell, because she would slow him down. He grabs his keys, and is crossing to the door when Etna drowsily asks, "Where are you going?"

At the threshold, James stops very briefly, but does not turn his head, does not look at his wife, and grips the keys hard, as if he were worried they would fall from his hands.

"Going hunting humans."

*

The boys ride their bikes down the street to the McDonald's on San Ysidro Boulevard. Omarr already regrets coming with them. He can hear his mother arguing with him. Even if he was only friends with Josh and David sometimes, that doesn't mean they won't influence his behavior. *You are who you associate with.* And he already feels ashamed that he gave in so quickly. A good person, like Zelia, wouldn't have given in so quickly. So, he realizes that this is it. Once he enjoys this milkshake with the boys, they will part ways, and he will not hang out with them ever again. He just needs to figure out how to avoid them, when he sees them in school, or around the neighborhood.

"What's going on?" David says, as they roll into the parking lot.

"Yeah, look," says Josh. "The window is busted."

The McDonald's looks different, for sure. The windows are cracked in several places, and some have a spray of cracks that emanate from a center, like a hole. They can't see inside.

And then they hear what sounds like fireworks, maybe from inside.

"What the fuck?" says Josh. And Omarr sighs. He's already cussing. He knows he shouldn't be here with them.

Suddenly, David yells, "Omarr!"

Omarr looks to David, who is jumping back on his bike while staring wide-eyed behind him. Omarr looks over to whatever is making David so scared. And then he sees him. It's Mr. Huberty. He's walking fast, right towards Omarr. And then Omarr sees that he has two of the guns from his house in both hands.

Josh yells, "Run!"

And all Omarr thinks is that Mr. Huberty is mad that he's hanging out with Josh and David, that he's associating with the wrong people. Mr. Huberty wouldn't want Zelia associating with the wrong people. Omarr waves his hands in front of him, and says, "They're not my friends, Mr. Huberty. I swear."

But Mr. Huberty keeps approaching, like he hasn't even heard Omarr. If only Mr. Huberty can hear that he really means it, because now Omarr *does* really mean it. It was a mistake to be here with them. He will not hang out with Josh and David anymore. Ever.

"Please, Mr. Huberty. I swear."

But Mr. Huberty doesn't respond, except to lift his right arm, the one that Omarr noticed twitched at dinner, but it was not twitching now, and in that hand is one of his small guns, like the ones police officers use, and he keeps walking, his eyes fixed, and Omarr knows he failed, and Omarr grips his bike, as Mr. Huberty gets close enough that Omarr can see Mr. Huberty's fury, can see his eye wall.

GETHSEMANE

So, this is the house I'm most excited to show you. It's a real jewel of the neighborhood. Built in 1900, it is what they call the Stick Eastlake style. You know what that is? It's Victorian. I have no idea why it's called Stick, though, but this is definitely Victorian—not one of those knock-offs trying to look Victorian with the prefab gingerbread you see in the suburbs of Atlanta, or Western Massachusetts. This is the real deal. All original exterior crownings. Real wood. Look at this porch! Isn't it something? And the stoop here? All marble finishes. Watch your step coming up.

What an entrance, right? And this isn't even the living room. In these turn-of-the-century places, there was always a receiving room. Some people refer to it as a parlor? Of course, we don't have that kind of ceremony, anymore, where we call upon people with cards, and need to figure out if hats and gloves stay on or are removed in-hand. Now, we shake, we hug. So sweet, isn't it? How intimate we've become? And now this space has no purpose, really. It's a bonus room. Think of what you can do with it! Everyone likes a bonus.

The hardwood is refurbished walnut and ash throughout—none of that pine nonsense that gets all dinged, slashed, gashed up, gutted. Ash is what they make baseball bats from. Kid-proof. If you have kids, you won't have to worry about them dropping dishes or scraping up the floor with their toys. Ah, no kids yet? But do you want them? How long have you two been together? Ten years? Well, it'll happen, when the time is right. I'm sure you all are so busy. Careers, am I right?

Look at these ceilings. 11 feet 3 inches on the first floor. Doesn't it make the rooms look even bigger? And this living room is to die for. Perfect for entertaining. I always prefer an oblong shape for parties, don't you? That way not everyone has to face one another; so awkward. That over there is a fully functioning fireplace. It's original, and except when the previous owners blocked it up—don't get me started on that—has burned wood for over 100 years. Isn't that something? Imagine how many pieces of wood have burned up in that thing? And what else? Pocket lint, gum wrappers, discarded mail, postcards, receipts, letters from old lovers, important tax documents, divorce papers. Thank God for fire, right?

The kitchen is a real centerpiece of this house. Completely updated, modern, all granite countertops. The island? Oh, that's not original. None of this kitchen is original, actually. But this is way better, you know, the modern kitchen design? The open concept flowing right into the dining room is Zen, gives you good Chi. So much better than those old, dark, closed in boxes that kitchens used to be. You know, those old kitchens were made like that to prevent fire from spreading too fast. You can imagine why that would be a big deal. Like, half of all our great cities were destroyed by blazes right around the same time kitchens were integrated with the main house: the Great Chicago Fire of 1871, the Boston fire a year later, the 1906 earthquake fire that ended just down the street from here, the sewing factory fires in New York City, not to mention the one in Wisconsin that killed a whole township. Imagine how many people burned up in those things, how many bodies jumped from upper-story windows, only to shatter their organs on pavement below. They didn't want to smell their flesh searing in the heat. Hell, I'd jump too.

When I was a little girl, I was terrified by the stove. No cooking for me. Oh, it was one of those things, you know, where one diddly memory will just ruin the whole shebang forever. I was trying to cook pancakes for my mother's birthday, I must have been six. It was a small Cape Cod in New Jersey, white with black shutters. So typical. And, silly me, I didn't know how to cook pancakes, but I was certain I could learn simply by looking at the pictures in the cookbook. As you can expect, I had flour everywhere. On the floor, all over the counter, in my hair. My father came home that morning—he worked the night shift at the trucking company—and saw the mess, like the whole kitchen had been whited out. You know he was tired. When he grabbed my hand and stuck it on the burner I hadn't felt anything that sharp before. I had been stung by a bee, and had sprained my ankle playing freeze tag with my brothers, but nothing like this. A burn doesn't feel like what you think; it's more like a bread knife slicing your hand. And the smell? Like charcoal and hair in a curling iron, something like that. I remember the smell more than anything. To this day I still can't abide the scent of a barbeque grill. Isn't it funny how a single memory can do that to you? You know he was tired. My father. Imagine coming home to that kind of mess after a long, grueling shift. I could never do a job that required me to work nights. Could you?

Just through this hallway is the master bedroom. You can see that a lot of care was taken to make this the epitome of luxury. When they refurbished the home they added the en-suite bathroom. Look at this 62-inch stone resin freestanding bathtub. What a dream. Imagine after a long day at the office coming home to this beauty. Light some candles, pour yourself a glass of pinot. Calgon, take me away! The double sink is a clever touch I particularly like. A must for a couple, to keep the marriage happy, am I right? And there is a rainfall shower with three heads. See, it comes from the top and from the sides. Look at this water pressure. And, big enough for two, to keep the marriage happy, am I right? With this shower, you'll have kids in no time!

This bedroom gets the best light. South-facing, with no bulkheads. One of the great things about San Francisco Victorians are the bay windows. The ones in this room are so deep you could have a little sitting area. Throw some pillows on it, grab a book, a perfect reading nook. This room is so much brighter than it was before the renovation. It was sad how dark the former owners kept it. They had painted it a navy blue. With brocade curtains, closed all the time. Can you imagine? Of course, the old man who died of cancer in this room probably wasn't interested in seeing much of the outside. It took six years to take him. The esophagus. It couldn't have been pleasant, the malignancy slowly lumping around his throat, cells replicating until it choked out his ability to swallow, sort of like marbles globbing his gullet until all he could do was pull blended Brussel sprouts through a straw. And then the metastasis, to his lungs, the white mutated nodes pulling on his alveoli like a boat anchor. Inhaling was a slow dry rattle, but exhaling was wet, like stewing molasses, until both stopped altogether, and there was only the body on the bed, and brocade curtains and closed out light. This bed? No, silly! This is all staging. His two grandkids, the ones who inherited the place, sold the bed in an estate sale, along with everything else. It was one of those lovely four-poster mahogany ones, but it had deep scratches on the headboard—have no idea where those came from, almost looked like animal claws. Such a lovely piece of craftsmanship. You'd think one of the grandkids would want to keep it, but maybe the scratches told them something they didn't want to remember, or maybe they suggested something about the mystery of their grandfather. And the bed, like mystery—Hell, like memory!—could never be fully theirs, anyway.

Now, this staircase. Isn't it dramatic? I love the way it ascends up to the second floor like a bird tilting westwards. Of course, it isn't the original staircase, which would have been located along the parlor wall, like most Stick Victorians. It had already been removed when we bought the place. We had to completely replace the stairs. Can you believe that this house was turned into a church for a while? Gethsemane Baptist. Can you imagine? And Gethsemane obviously didn't have much success in the way of a donation bucket, know what I mean? And not much imagination, either! They built these little clapper steps in the back by the kitchen, to make more space for the congregation room. Super narrow, just plywood boards. Who knows what they did with the staircase they removed. Probably a rich maple railing. It's such a shame. You can just imagine how much a church setup would have ruined the architectural integrity of this place. It took so much ingenuity for the flippers to restore it back to any semblance of its original glory, what, with all the cut-ups and wall-chops. And what did the church do with the stairs? Look, I have nothing against making a house of God wherever you please, but could they not use a little inspiration when they remodeled—if you can call it that—for worship? You should have seen how they gutted this baby. I'd show you pictures, but it'd ruin you for life, I tell you. Sure, the church was poor and needed to make do, but you don't have to be rich to see the beauty in things, am I right? Can I get an Amen?

The second floor has three full bedrooms and two full baths, all with ample closet space, polished hardwood floors, and newly installed recessed lighting. This one on the left, though, is the most charming. Isn't this adorable? The window alcoves are just precious. This was definitely a child's room, for multiple generations even. When we first inspected the place the walls were purple, and then when we began stripping we discovered Laura Ingalls Wilder wallpaper, you know those *Little House* books? Apparently, that wallpaper was all the rage in the 40's, so this must have been a girl's room through the ages. It's not a big room, but the closet is disproportionately large. Big enough to hide a full-grown woman, yes? In fact, that is exactly what it did, in various instances, from September 1951 to March 1952. Sophie Mears, wife of Ernest, began to hide in this closet when her husband would come home drunk, convinced his lovely, amply built wife was sleeping with other men while he was out looking for work. He lost his job at the shipyard when the industry slowed down after the war, and it made him mean, you know, in that way that men were allowed to be back then. The very first time he came home drunk with the accusations, Sophie sported a generous shiner around her left eye that Ernest said guaranteed no man would look twice at her. It was their daughter, Rosie, who suggested her closet as a hiding spot. And it worked. Ernest never did find her in there before he'd pass out, his anger always quitting once he fell asleep, but not before he stumbled around the house yelling her name, turning over chairs and slamming drawers. Sophie made a little nest of blankets and coats on the closet floor for these nights. It wasn't too bad, at the end of the day. And when Ernest left for job-hunting in the morning, Rosie opened the closet door, and Sophie crawled out and made her and her daughter their ritual biscuits and scrambled eggs. Not a bad little cubby spot, huh?

Take a look at this attic. Isn't it spectacular? The roof pitch goes up to nine feet at the center, so there's lots of space to turn this into an office or study, maybe even a craft room. Unfortunately, because of the angle of the roof, the square footage can't be included in the overall appraisal of the home. According to the American National Standards Institute, square footage can only be calculated if over half of the floor space is met with ceilings of at least seven feet. So, even though this is a functional 450 square foot room, the roof slant makes the room just shy of meeting that requirement. Isn't that a shame? This standard is the reason why we don't build houses like this anymore, with this kind of dramatic pitch. But this definitely served as a bedroom back in the day. In fact, two folks met their bedridden death here: a woman during childbirth in 1908, and a little boy in 1919, Spanish Flu. Did you know more people died of flu in 1919 than from the Great War? The woman and the boy were not related. Wouldn't that have been tragic if they were? What a good story that would make. Now, don't you go stealing my idea! That's one for Hollywood!

Take a look at those beams. I bet you're wondering—because you would be absolutely right; those indeed *are* redwood. In fact, the whole house frame is redwood. It's the most durable. Many San Francisco houses were framed in it, especially before everyone got all environmental. The wood is naturally fire resistant—did you know that?—and is virtually termite and rot-proof. It's the perfect material for building a city. But back then, it wasn't an easy task to fell one of these giants, when all they had were men and axes. These are the tallest trees in the world, 300 feet tall, a dozen feet wide. The loggers would basically chop a pie wedge into the base of the tree, with the bottom cut perfectly horizontal. Then, to guarantee the tree fell in the right direction, they'd make sure the back of the face cut was perfectly perpendicular to the direction of the fall. Can you imagine getting the calculations on that wrong? Even just a hair off and that tree would fall over a hundred miles per hour across the forest floor. And, *splat*.

Speaking of *splat*, a man sure did felling the very tree that frames this house, including this beam here. His name was Burt Tyler. He was twenty-one, with his first baby on the way. He and Dorothy moved from Indiana four months prior, lured by the logging boom. Sure enough, he was resting for lunch, smoking a freshly rolled-up cigarette on an old stump, when he heard screams from high up the hill, grown men shrieking high-pitched like women, and then the familiar thunder-crack of the tree splintering before the fall. You'd think it would have happened in slow-motion, you know, like the movies? But all Burt caught was the sound, then the metallic chill of his own veins, and then a flash of darkness, the hurled body of the giant tree blocking out the sun just before the more permanent darkness. And the other trees in the grove screamed, as well. No kidding! I'm serious! Redwoods have shallow roots, but they creep along the forest floor for hundreds of feet. And, different trees will link their roots together, like they're all holding hands forming a chain. Biologists know now that once they intertwine, they communicate with one another, a sort of telepathy. So, when one tree is cut, they all feel it. And when we are cut, we scream. So. Isn't that something? Screaming trees.

Have you seen the redwoods? No?! They are a must-see if you're moving to Northern California. So impressive. Muir Woods is nice, but really touristy, lots of fanny packs and selfie sticks. I recommend going south to Big Basin in the Santa Cruz mountains. Much less people, you can really take some terrific pictures without being photo-bombed. No filter, am I right?

Watch your step coming on to the back porch. Isn't this nice? So private. No one can see you back here. A little oasis, yet everything just beyond the wall-high wood fence—the most current design in sound deflection technology. It's like you don't even live in a city, right? You can enjoy the perks of what urban neighborhoods offer without exposing yourself to the unseemly elements of, you know, *urban* neighborhoods, all while you enjoy your morning coffee.

Now, don't get me wrong. The neighborhood is very safe. Back in the day, maybe not so much. When this property served as Gethsemane Baptist, let's just be honest: it was rough. Thirty years ago, no one wanted to live here, except for the artists and the gays. Well, others *lived* here, but, *you know*. Well, I mean, people *did*. It just wasn't much of a market back then, is what I mean. Before the neighborhood was called NoPa, it was known as The Western Addition. Well, there still is a part of the city called the Western Addition, but that is way *over there*. It's so different than this part of town. But back when this was still part of the Western Addition…well, let's just say people like you wouldn't be looking for a home here, know what I mean? And such a shame, right? These homes are beautiful! So, when people began noticing the potential—again, the gays; they always have their pulse on what's hot, right? (my motto in real estate: invest wherever you see women walking around in combat boots, no matter how scary it is to drive through)—they thought to change the name of the neighborhood, to make it reflect the improvement taking place. I'm sure you know, there's power in a name. Renaming a thing does something to it. Born again Christians do it. Women do it when they get married. Slaves were renamed before they were sold. Of course, we don't do *that* anymore. Goodness.

Don't worry, between you and me, only the right element is moving in to this area. How do I know? The Dollar Store down the street closed, and the most adorable athleisure boutique moved in. On the corner, a gourmet coffee shop opened in an old auto-body garage. And did you see that really nice BBQ place opening across from the park, with the raw wood panels and the Edison bulbs hanging from the ceiling? It used to be this ratty old restaurant called Da Pit. Can you imagine naming your restaurant Da Pit? Who would want to go there? See, a name change has power.

The value of this property will only increase, I guarantee, so you can maximize your upward mobility when you decide to move on to the next best place, and then the next best place. They say that cashing out here will be smart in about three years, and then you can buy a house in West Oakland, or maybe even in Portland or Austin outright with the profit! You could even do what we did here and flip it—a little gingerbread here and there—and make a killing. I mean, that's what real estate is, right? A chance to build equity? A killing.

Oh, don't let the graffiti unnerve you. It's merely vestiges of what this place was. I know what it says, but you can't be intimidated by meager threats. Besides, they don't know you personally, that you're really nice people working for a living, just like everyone else. I mean, isn't that tag sort of reverse racism? Don't you think that's a bit hypocritical? You know, so many people resist progress, even if the change benefits them. This neighborhood is so much safer now. And, there's lots of great restaurants and shops. Before, we're talking just ten years ago, no one visited this neighborhood. It was full of places that only the locals frequented. There was no allure, no intrigue, only *people.* If you're going to buy property, you want it to be a destination, right?

The former residents? Oh, you can't be thinking about that. I can tell you, the people who owned this house are lucky they could sell it in the first place, considering the shape it was in. And, they got a pretty penny, way more than they paid for it. They probably bought a big house in Antioch or one of those other outer Bay Area suburbs, probably welcomed the change to something quieter. They probably are swimming in their newly installed backyard saltwater pool right now. They wanted to leave. We didn't put a gun to their head.

Now, c'mon, we're here about *your* future. That's how it works, right?

FOOTFALL

Corey had never gone this far into the woods before, this far past the fort, past the ridgetop, towards the next valley over. He could tell there were redwoods at the bottom, could see their stubby branches rise atop the canopy. That would mean there was a creek down there, and the ground would be soft and orange with pine needles, giant ferns, the valley quiet. He wanted to go all the way down, but decided against it. While it was afternoon up near the top of the ridge, and the sun still high, by the time he got down it would be getting too close to dusk, and the valley floor much darker. If he was going to be out this late, he had to stick close to the fort. He needed the higher ground in case the fugitive spotted him first.

The wind on the ridge drowned out the helicopters, but Corey knew they were still out there, had been for two days and nights. His stepdad said they wouldn't stop circling until they found the fugitive, even though it was Saturday. The fugitive had killed a man a long time ago, had broken a guard's arm to escape Pelican Bay on Thursday, and was considered dangerous. The TV said he might even have a weapon.

Corey was grateful for the news. It took everyone's mind off him, when every day this past week he was called names at school, and the boys behind him made kissy noises on the bus, and his stepdad came home from the penitentiary and looked at Corey like a flat tire on the side of the road. When his stepdad told Corey's mother about the fugitive on Thursday, she hugged herself and said, "What is the world coming to?" She asked that about a lot of things. Corey hoped she didn't ask his stepdad that about him. He didn't want to think about that, though.

He thought instead about the mission. He began at the fort, then circled around, a bit more each time, until he did a full reconnaissance of both sides of the ridge, never losing sight of where he started. Corey pretended that his best friend Mikey was alongside carrying his Hobo knife, surveying the ridge. He pushed his BB gun strap farther onto his back, squatted down against a stand of trees, and pointed to a small clearing. "See over there? Fresh campsite. Maybe six hours old." Corey imagined Mikey shade his eyes like a visor and say, "Looks like the enemy's heading east. Let's head back to base, for better visibility."

Back at the fort, Corey climbed up and sat at the edge of the platform, built between the two larger branches of the sycamore. The leaf coverage was still good, and Mikey had taught Corey what clothes to wear so he looked like a shadow in the trees. He stayed in this spot and watched, just like he did after school yesterday, until the sun went down. Mikey also taught Corey how to listen for animals in the woods, their footfall on the forest floor, the difference between deer and black bears, between fox and bobcats. He pretended Mikey was with him, that they spotted a mountain lion, and launched pine cones like they were grenades. He imagined Mikey had painted their faces green and black, to blend in. They planned to be army men for Halloween. He imagined, as they listened for snapping twigs and other forest floor crackle, that Mikey whispered he was sorry for telling on him. Corey pretended that when they spent the night in the fort last weekend, they curled up in their sleeping bags and fell asleep like normal, that Corey didn't roll towards Mikey and kiss him on the lips, and that Mikey didn't go quiet the rest of the night and next morning, and then make fun of him on the playground when they were back at school.

The day was getting almost to the point of purple when Corey heard a rustle from far behind him. He moved to the other side of the fort's platform, and looked out. He wasn't sure what kind of animal it was, too soft to be a bear, too steady to be much else. At first, he heard only the rhythmic crackle, but then saw glimpses of movement deep in the layers of trees, traveling down from the ridgetop. He whispered to Mikey, "Fifty yards, southwest." As the movement came closer Corey could see flashes of black, but he wasn't sure if it was fur or shadow. Then, a sound came from the creature. A cough.

Corey silently climbed down the ladder of the fort, careful not to scrape the BB gun on the wood planks. He took one last look at the direction in which the figure was moving, and crept towards its path. Mikey had taught him to always follow behind, because bears had eyes in front and deer had eyes on the side. He stayed far back, trying to step with the figure to hide his own footfall.

For a moment Corey thought about quitting the hunt and going home. What if this was the fugitive and he heard Corey behind him? What if he was dangerous and broke Corey's arm? He hesitated and thought he could make it just in time for dinner if he turned around, but then told himself that if he was ever going to prove to Mikey and his schoolmates, to his stepdad, that he wasn't a sissy, he had to keep going. If he found the fugitive and reported it to his stepdad, maybe wrestle him down or maim him with a BB, Corey could be a hero, and the whole fifth grade class would forget about what happened last weekend. Even Mikey would be friends with him again. He increased the speed of his steps, and kept his eyes on the man in front of him.

The man was not in an orange jumpsuit, as Corey imagined, but in a black hooded sweatshirt and dark blue Dickies. Strands of dirty blonde hair poked out the sides. Corey didn't know what color hair the fugitive had, because the mugshot they showed on TV was of a man with a buzzcut. The more distance he gained on the man, the more he noticed the man limping, his left arm crossing over to the right leg, the one he favored. Corey also heard soft grunting from the man. Was he tired? Was he hurt? Did one of the prison guards break his arm, too? He imagined his stepdad running after the prisoner, deep into the woods, with his pistol drawn. His stepdad wouldn't be afraid. He'd have caught up with him, aimed and shot him down to the ground without even a second of doubt. Corey knew his stepdad wasn't a sissy, and this is why Corey kept following the man, even though it was getting dark.

The man's grunting seemed to be getting louder, his pace slower. Corey could even make out a few bad words that the man muttered, the dark of the forest making the sounds clearer. And then, the man stumbled towards a stand of quivering aspen and slid down the trunk of the biggest tree.

For a while Corey crouched down behind a felled ponderosa and listened. He couldn't hear much of anything except the warblers high up in the canopy and the man's heavy breathing. He tried to slow his own, to not give himself away, but it was difficult, and blood pounded in his ears. Night had almost fully come, and some stars were peeking from the deep blue above the ridge, but Corey's eyes adjusted and he could see the man clearly. He looked younger than his stepdad, with a pale face. There was a tattoo on the side of his neck, which Corey didn't remember seeing in the TV mugshot. Other than breathing heavy, the man was not doing much else. One hand clutched his side, while the other lay splayed on the ground. Corey lifted his BB gun and released the safety. It was already loaded, and Corey could see the BB in position give off the slightest bit of glint. He inched closer, the blood loud in his head.

As he crept into the clearing, Corey could make out more of the man, broad shoulders, big hands, but thin, like a swimmer. He knew that if he had to, home was exactly to his right, maybe two miles or so, and if the man made any sudden move, he'd shoot and take off running. He pretended Mikey was with him, ready to back him up with a knife jab, and they'd bound together, somehow the sound of both their boots a better thing.

"Hey kid," the man said, a strained voice.

Corey stopped, said nothing, kept his BB gun ready. *Thirty feet, north by northwest*, he pretended to whisper to Mikey. He saw that the man was bleeding from his side. Even in the growing darkness, the blood shone against the black sweatshirt.

"You can put the gun down. I'm not going to hurt you." The man pulled his hand from his side and held it up, covered in blood. He dropped it back down and murmured something Corey couldn't hear.

"You that fugitive on the news?" Corey hated how high-pitched his voice sounded.

The man laughed, "Fugitive?" Then, he coughed, hacked up and spit without moving his head. "You by chance have something to eat on you?"

Corey wondered if he should get home now and tell his parents, call the police. He was about to take off back to the trailer park, but realized the man might get up and run someplace else by the time Corey got into Gasquet. Maybe people wouldn't believe he actually found the man, accuse Corey of making the whole thing up. Mikey would know what to do if he were here. Mikey would suggest they hog-tie him. Corey didn't have any rope with him. Mikey would have brought rope, because he was like that. Mikey wasn't ever called a sissy. Corey could shoot the fugitive to keep him there, but he knew he wouldn't. And that's what made him a sissy.

"I have a fruit roll-up," Corey said, and pulled it from his pocket.

"If you don't mind," said the man.

"What's wrong with you? You shot or something?"

The man laughed, until he coughed.

Corey thought if he could show his stepdad and the police something of the fugitive, they'd believe him, even if the man did run off and hide. "If you want this roll-up, you gotta give me something. You know, in return."

The man smiled like he was going to laugh again, stared at Corey for a long moment, and then pulled a chain off his neck. "Here," and threw it towards Corey. It landed a couple feet from his boot. Corey threw the fruit roll-up, and the man leaned to the right and caught it with his hand, but only after a horrible yelp. He was in pain. Corey quickly picked up the chain, stuffed it in his pocket.

Corey hurried back to the fort to grab his pack. Instead of heading straight home, he traced his steps back to the fugitive, careful not to make noise, in case the man had run off and now was hiding. Maybe the man wasn't as hurt as he looked, and would chase him down, hold him hostage. Corey couldn't let that happen. He prepped his BB gun as he approached the stand of aspen, looking out for the black sweatshirt. It was pretty dark out now.

The man was still there, in the same spot, sitting against the tree, his breathing heavy, looking up at the treetops, like he was praying. Thirty feet away, Corey unzipped his pack. The man's head quickly turned, but he didn't jump up or even scurry backward. "Kid?"

"Yeah," Corey said. He fished the water canteen out of his pack, crept up ten feet closer, and then tossed it to the man. It landed a couple of feet from his left boot with a dull thud. Then, Corey took off running, back home.

It took longer than he thought, the dark full on when he walked into the asphalt clearing of the trailer park. As he turned the corner, Corey saw his stepdad's pickup, the lights on in the kitchen. When he opened the door, he immediately caught the smell of boiling hot dogs, and the yeast of beer before sight of the Bud Light cans on the kitchen table. His stepdad was rolling a quarter on his knuckles. His mother was standing at the sink, pulling seeds out of a small pumpkin.

"Just in time for dinner, honey," she said to Corey, and showed her work. "Look what I got at the farm stand in Adam's Station?"

When Corey didn't say anything, his mother brought her hand up to the fresh bruise on her neck.

"It's for Halloween. Don't you think it'll be nice to carve a face in it?"

She tried to give him a smile, and went back to the sink and seed-pulling. Corey followed her, gave her a hug from behind, and turned to the boiling hot dogs. He skewered one with a fork, and ate it while he watched his mother wash the insides of the pumpkin. When he finished he scooted next to his mother, washed the fork, and watched her dry the inside. Corey thought it would be the first thing he mentioned when he got home, but now he didn't know if he should say anything about the man in the woods. It wasn't the right time.

Corey didn't know his stepdad had stood up and was staring at him with the dull eyes that the beer drinking did.

"What's that around your neck, son?"

"Nothing," Corey said. "Just something I found in the woods."

"Is that a necklace, Corey?" his stepdad asked.

Corey didn't say anything. His mother stopped fussing with the pumpkin, and froze, like a deer in the woods. Corey looked down at the kitchen linoleum.

"Who gave you that?"

Corey shook his head.

"What, are you wearing it to be pretty?"

Corey shook his head.

"Pretty for Mikey?"

"Alan, please," his mother said.

"You wanna go and kiss him again?"

"Alan! Stop!"

Corey ran to his bedroom and closed the door. He ripped the chain off and threw it against the wall. At first he only heard muffled voices on the other side of the wall, but then his stepdad's voice got louder.

"He's not a kid, anymore, Jennifer! He's gonna get his ass kicked!"

In between was his mother's voice, but he couldn't make out what she said.

"You have to stop babying him!"

More of his mother's muffles.

"You want him to grow up a faggot?!"

And then Corey heard the sound that made him hide under his covers. He imagined grabbing his BB gun, ripping the bedroom door open, aiming square at the spot between his stepdad's eyebrows, and saying some one-liner like heroes did in the movies. Mikey would say something like that. Mikey wouldn't hide under the covers until he fell asleep.

When he came out of his room the next morning, his stepdad was gone. His mother was carving the pumpkin with a steak knife. She was almost finished with the mouth, working on a boxy tooth on the bottom. There was a new bruise on her neck, and one on her wrist. When she noticed him, his mother lifted the pumpkin and asked, "Whaddya think?" Corey didn't say anything, but nodded. He poured himself some cereal.

"Want to help me decorate? I've got some cotton for spider webs, and plastic bats to go in the corners."

Corey didn't say anything, kept eating his cereal.

"You can carve the eyes and nose."

"I was gonna go to the fort."

"Come on. It'll be fun."

Corey finished his cereal, washed the bowl and spoon, and went to his room and grabbed his coat. When he returned his mother was biting her bottom lip. "You know, you can at least help me clean up a little bit before Alan gets home."

"But Mom..."

"And I don't like you going out in the woods when that convict is out there."

Corey stood still, between his mother and the front door.

"Why were you wearing that necklace, Corey? You can't get him mad like that."

"It's not a necklace."

"Here, help me string this cotton."

The crunch of his stepdad's tires came just as Corey and his mother finished hanging the spider webs. Some of the bats were nestled in the batting, some on top of the porch railing, the coffee table. The pumpkin was carved, with lopsided eyes that looked more silly than scary. "Now, we just need to find a candle," his mother said, just as his stepdad walked through the door.

"Tah-dah!" his mother exclaimed.

Corey's stepdad was cheerful. "It looks great in here."

"Me and Corey did it." His mother grasped her hands in front like some of the girls did in Corey's school.

His stepdad pulled a box out of his pocket. It was wrapped with a silver ribbon. He gave it to his mother. "For me?" She opened it, and inside was a thin silver necklace with a small green pendant in the shape of a tear drop.

"Alan, I love emeralds!"

"I know. That's why I got it."

"It's beautiful!"

His mother pulled the necklace out of the box and unclasped it.

"Here," his stepdad said, and took the necklace and hung it around his mother's neck, and kissed her hair.

His mother laid her fingers on the pendant, "Isn't it beautiful?"

"I'm glad you like it. It wasn't cheap."

"It's so thoughtful." His mother looked to Corey. "Don't you think?"

His stepdad wrapped his arms around his mother's waist from

behind and rested his chin on her shoulder. "See. *Girls* wear necklaces, Corey."

"Isn't it nice, Corey?"

"I think I'll go outside," Corey said softly and, while his parents cooed over one another, he slipped out of the trailer, and walked into the woods. He wished he brought his BB gun, but didn't want to risk taking the time to go back into the trailer and into his bedroom. He thought he would walk to the fort, and maybe creep to the stand of aspens, see if the man was still there. He needed to get his canteen back.

The man was in the exact same spot. Same tree, same black hoodie and dark blue Dickies. Corey's canteen was resting on the man's lap. The man was dead.

Corey crouched on the ground some feet away from the body. He could tell the man was dead, because his eyes weren't all the way closed, and his chest didn't move. Other than that, he looked like he was sleeping, like he had too many beers and fell asleep sitting on the couch, like his stepdad did some nights.

After staring awhile at the body, Corey stood up, brushed the bottom of his pants off, and crept backward, like a bobcat. He untied his shoes, pulling the laces out of the eyelets. He pretended that Mikey was with him, that he and Mikey spotted the fugitive and concocted a plan to sneak up on him while he slept. "I'll hold him down while you do his hands, then we'll do his feet."

Corey moved in a big circle around the body and then slinked up behind. He grabbed the man's wrists, pulled them onto his lap, and tied one shoelace into a double-knot. He checked to make sure it was tight enough so the prisoner couldn't escape. "He can't wiggle out of that."

Corey then used the other shoelace to tie the man's ankles. The lace was barely long enough, but he managed to make one knot. He checked for slack. "Good enough," he said to Mikey. "He won't be going anywhere."

The man appeared peaceful, even though he was tied up, like someone who needed sleep and found it. Corey looked at the slope of his shoulders, the stubble on his face. He brought one of his fingers up to the fugitive's chin to feel it. Sandpaper, but softer. He saw a small tuft of sandy hair peeking out the top of his hoodie. He touched the spot and felt the hairs. Then he pressed his whole hand, and slid it down, inside the hoodie. It wasn't as cold as he thought it would be, but it wasn't warm either. He felt the mounds of the man's chest. It was hairy. Corey moved his hand along the hair, back and forth, slowly, several times, and then back up the neck. He looked up to the sky, took a deep breath, and pulled his hand away.

"Let's make sure these bindings are secure," he said to Mikey. He checked the ties at the hands, then at the ankles. He decided to make the ankle ties tighter, and used all his strength to favor enough shoelace for a double-knot. By the time Corey finished, the sun was falling behind the ridge. "We'll carry the fugitive to justice come light, Commander Mike. For now, let's rest."

In the morning the living room coffee table was full of Bud Light cans, too many to count. His mother was standing at the counter staring at nothing but the sink. She was pale and her hair was un-brushed and stringy. His stepdad was laying in his arms on the kitchen table. Corey had heard them laughing and singing from beyond his bedroom walls most of the night, until he managed to fall asleep. The coffee maker was making its bubbling sound while it percolated.

"Corey, son," his stepdad said, "me and your mother are moving a little slow today."

"Are you guys sick?" Corey asked.

"Sort of," his stepdad laughed, "her more than me."

Corey's mother was still staring at the sink but was smiling. She looked like she was remembering something funny, seeing it like it was far away, or long ago. Her face made Corey feel sad, though. The coffee maker kept sputtering.

Corey watched them, his stepdad's head back on his arms, his mother's hair limp around her face. The room smelled like sugar and bread and sweat. He was going to pour himself a bowl of cereal, but the smell of the kitchen killed his hunger. He thought about today's mission in the woods, and how he and Mikey would haul the fugitive into Gasquet on a wagon, ride him through the main street, push open the doors of the Sheriff's office, and claim the reward money. He would buy himself a pair of cowboy boots with spurs on the back, and Mikey would buy a BB gun so they both had one. Corey would also buy his mother a car so she and his stepdad didn't have to share.

As if she was aware he was thinking about her, Corey's mother turned around to look at him.

"Baby, could you get my cigarettes from the truck?"

He went out and climbed into the pickup, fished his hand into the passenger door compartment. His mother always left her Newports there. He pulled them out and inspected the box, partially crushed. None of the cigarettes were damaged. He popped out of the truck and looked at the sky. A cool blue. A bit of fog pulling away from the coast like cotton batting, sparse and drifting above the rising hills. School was going to be really hard tomorrow.

"I think I found the escaped convict," he said, when he returned.

His stepdad was now reading something on his phone, and without looking up said, "Yeah, don't worry. The county has their chopper, and the Highway Patrol donated theirs. He won't get too far."

"He's in the woods, up on the ridge."

His mother was pouring the freshly brewed coffee in the faded Dollywood mug she always drank out of. "That's why I don't want you going out there, Corey, not until they find him. He's dangerous."

"I found him."

Corey's stepdad rocked a little in his chair. "Is that so?"

He puffed up his chest, and with his best impression of Mikey's voice, Corey said, "I'm going to bring in the fugitive."

"You do that," a slight glow of the smartphone reflecting on his stepdad's eyeballs.

"Where are your shoelaces, Corey?" his mother asked, the crease in between her eyebrows folded together.

Corey looked down, didn't say anything.

"Honey?"

Corey shrugged.

"Answer your mother," his stepdad said. Corey looked over at him. He wasn't staring at the phone any more, but straight at him, the morning slow all but gone. Corey could see his wildness return.

"I'm sure it's fine," his mother said, but to whom Corey didn't know. She was looking at a space between him and his stepdad.

"Well?" His stepdad sat up in his chair, pulled forward like a dog watching a stick.

"I found him," Corey said.

"Where are your fucking shoelaces, Corey?"

Corey felt the tears begin, and all he wished for was that they wouldn't.

"It's not a big deal, Alan."

His stepdad quickly jumped to his feet. "Yes, it is, Jennifer. This is exactly what *is* a big deal." He turned to Corey, pointed his finger towards him. "If you've managed to lose your shoelaces, have the balls to own up, son."

Corey ran to his room. Behind him he heard his mother say things he's heard before. Their voices rose and collided beyond the walls, until he couldn't make out anything either of them said. He grabbed his BB gun, tucked it tight to his body, took a deep breath, and quickly ran out of the room and out the front door.

Behind him he heard his mother say, "Where are you going?"

Corey ran all the way to the stand of aspen, as fast as he could. The forest was silent, except for a few birds high in the canopy, but the blood in his head was loud and his breathing scratchy.

The man looked the same, in the same spot, sitting the same way, only now the skin of his face and hands more ashy, less pink, a bit puffy. Corey slumped down on his knees a few feet in front, his breathing heavy from running and crying. He wished Mikey was here, because he would know what to do. Mikey always knew what to do. He would ask Mikey, "How can I be more like you?" But he knew he could never ask Mikey that question, even if he and Mikey were still friends. But he also knew that he and Mikey would never be friends again. His stepdad was right. He was a sissy.

Corey took off the safety of the BB gun, cocked it and brought the butt to the square of his right shoulder. Mikey had taught him how to shoot. He aimed the rifle at the fugitive's head. He imagined he and Mikey dragging the fugitive to the police station. Corey would be wearing his new boots to school. He pulled the trigger. The BB sank into the fugitive's cheek and disappeared behind a small dark hole, some small flies escaping the mouth. Corey cocked the rifle. He imagined his name all over news feeds, his name and Mikey's, the heroes of Gasquet, bringing the fugitive to justice. Corey pulled the trigger. The BB hit right between the eyes, and the man's head jerked a bit. Corey cocked the rifle. He recalled the hair of the man's chest on his fingers, his skin, and Corey began to cry again. He brought the butt of the rifle to the square of his shoulder, just as Mikey had taught him. He imagined being interviewed on the news, the reporter asking him how he found the fugitive, how he was brave enough to capture him in the woods. And, Corey, about to answer, but knowing he doesn't want to answer without Mikey. His eyes search for him. And now Mikey is next to him, and they answer the reporter's questions, and Mikey smiles at the reporters and then back at Corey. And then his stepdad is in the crowd behind the reporter, and his mother, too, and the whole fifth-grade class, all of Gasquet, looking to the hero. Corey aimed again, his breath and blood a single thing, and pulled the trigger.

FAULTLINE: COFFEE SPILLED

The café is a worn, warm storefront on a stretch of street in the deep pocket of change, that used to be deemed unseemly with its whiff of raw fish heads and burnt pinto beans, with its car horns yelling across corners, with its hand-painted signs above doors, with its paint cracking, that used to be bedroom quiet in the darkest part of night, that used to be a haven for whispered drug deals. But now the drug deals are done inside, and the whispers are of lovers making deals, and the street narrowed, and our eyes widened.

The story goes like this: coffee spills. The woman who ordered the coffee is, by all accounts, lovely. She wears a sundress that drapes on her body modestly, but with terrific suggestion that her body is under this cotton floral print, and has the potential to do things. And now, the coffee that has spilled seeps into that cotton right on her breasts, where you now can see the outline of them, the bottom curve where they bulb on her chest. The coffee is very hot. Everyone in the café knows this because the woman, incongruous with her pixie haircut, her soft, round cheeks, her glossy pink lips, her linen lace-up Espadrilles, screeches out a nasty, nasally "Fuck!" She bends forward, pulls on the top of her dress.

She says it again. "Fuck!" She looks wildly at the barista, a young man with a trimmed beard and a very thin, low-cut v-neck that flaunts his chest hair, this man who has stumbled against the counter and lost control of the freshly poured coffee that has spilled onto the pixie woman's sundress, and she says, "Fuck. You!"

There is another woman in the café. She is, to most, still considered young. Her daughter, with thin mousy brown hair identical to her mother's, sits across from her, and sees her mother's light blue eyes widen, watches her mother swing her head towards the pixie woman, who is still pulling the dress away from her chest in an awkward bend of her body. She says, "Excuse me. There is a child present." The daughter watches her mother's lips involuntarily tug towards her nose, and she might even call it a snarl, like that of a dog. Her mother was not a dog. She was usually calculated and muted, as if the animal instinct were rubbed out of her with sandpaper, and all that was left was a bone-smooth polish, her buffed fingernails reflecting little boxes of the window-light. The girl was too young to know of her mother's disappointments, all the lovers who had left, including her father, a schoolteacher who thought he wanted a child of his own—to practice his years of accrued insight—but who then realized he taught in a classroom because it was window-parenting, and that he more enjoyed a life that was outside looking in. The mother often envisions that the men leave because of the daughter, but then shakes her head violently to push the thought away. Yet it sits inside her, quietly breathing into the corners of whatever is left of her dreams. The mother packs up, rips out her keys, mumbling words like "crass" and "young" and "bitch", leaps out of the chair, and says, "Come on, Sabrina," then glares at the pixie woman—whom she notices has awkwardly knelt down in front of her daughter—and storms out of the shop. Sabrina grabs her mother's half-drunk coffee and follows out the door. "Mom, you forgot your coffee."

The mother swings around, and pulls hard on Sabrina's arm, "Come on!" The coffee spills onto the sidewalk. The force of the anger, the energy that brews in the mother's body and releases in the seethe of the command, and the grip of the fingers on flesh, is so pointed, so specific, that it travels into the girl, red finger-wide bruises bloom under her skin. The shock of the energy, the pain of its force, goes through Sabrina, the look of her mother's fury superimposed onto her memory like the atomic bomb silhouettes blasted onto concrete walls. That memory will eclipse so many others, even of more profound events, and will reveal itself several times in her adulthood, most often as she makes love to men she has grown fond of, and worries they will leave. It is in the heaviness of sex that the memory will emerge, as if from deep water—the image of her mother's small tight face, the grit of her mouth, the grip of her hand—and with that Sabrina will transmit the force of the memory onto her lover—his face flushed, damp with sweat—through her fingernails, pressing deeper into his chest, and pulling down, until a small line of blood blooms from his skin, and his eyes open and widen with the instinct of terror. *Stay with me*, she thinks.

But there is another story here, the one that is less often written. It is where the young hairy-chested barista, once he has realized his mistake, that the bottom of the coffee cup has nicked the edge of the counter and the coffee sails into the air, once he sees the pixie woman clutching the stained cotton of her sundress, before her shock coalesces into the ball of fury that releases into that very audible "fuck," that he looks at her with so much sorrow, a blue cold that spreads out from his heart, across his chest, that wants to wrap itself around the pixie woman, to shroud her in the apology that could cool the red hot of the spilled liquid, and the white hot of her anger.

There is the moment where the pixie woman, after she has screamed her shock and anger in the form of that "fuck," after she turns to the angry mutterings of the mousy-haired mother and notices the ten-year-old daughter staring out, eyes widened, sees the innocence of the girl and recognizes her painful desire to preserve it, something identical to shame, that she lowers herself down, level to Sabrina and says, "I'm so sorry, honey," but this is only after the mother has already grabbed her and rushed out the door.

And that instant the mother sees how her fingers have violated her daughter's flesh, much the way her once rigid and now fractured hopes have violated the precious little love that she still allows herself to feel, she becomes frightened for her daughter, the fear she will live in a world of little kindness, a world full of injury, and suddenly wraps her arms around Sabrina, picks her up with a strength that can only be summoned with the emotions of survival: either fear or love, but one can never see the difference in such small apertures, and Sabrina feels an instant of weightlessness, the burn of her mother's fingers forgotten in the cooling of her embrace.

And, finally, the tears of Sabrina, already falling as she punctures the lover's chest with her fingernails, the simultaneity of the anger and love raking his body, the urge to hurt and to hold, collapsed. And what of her lover? Which intent of hers does he understand first? Her fury, or her love? When his eyes widen in the violence, does he spread outward, or does he tighten into a hot white ball? And maybe, in this moment, Sabrina thinks *if only stories of forgiveness wrote themselves as urgently as stories of anger.* What would that mean for us all?

CLIPS

In this clip, the guys are throwing a football. The white one is in the foreground on the right, his broad back filling a third of the screen. He throws with ease, his biceps firm but not strained, and the pigskin sails across the frame, across a rock-and-sand landscape, a desert landscape, to the darker guy, maybe Spanish or Italian, somewhere Mediterranean. He allows the ball to land into the cradle of his arms, cupped at his barely-there belly, with a delicacy, a sensitivity that has me issue a slight breath. The Latin guy grins, the satisfaction of such a softness when nothing about the action should seem so, his mouth confident and easy, a grin that men learn when they grow up with a doting mother who insists that they can do no wrong, a grin that everyone understands is handsome, because we want men to believe they can do no wrong. And maybe by them believing it, they won't. If that were only true.

"We really should give them names," says Andre, nestled next to me, deep into our worn, paisley couch, a handful of popcorn covering his face, kernels dropping on his lap. It is early evening. He's in his pajamas, probably has been all day.

The handsome, grinning Latin guy throws the ball back to the white guy, whose face you can't see now but is his own version of handsome, only much more rugged, not nearly as man-boyish. He might be older, but you can never tell with white guys. Some look old even at thirty, cracks around their eyes, their forehead, their skin betraying them. A desert floor. This one has a buzz-cut, but you can assume he has blondish hair, and creases on each side of his mouth that could trap dirt. His catch of the ball isn't nearly as graceful, but he succeeds, and immediately throws it back.

Once the ball is in flight, the white guy runs; you can see the power of his legs pushing against the fatigues as he sprints towards the Latin guy, who just caught the ball and is grinning again, his upper body leaning forward. He begins shuffling side-to-side, the top of his head like a battering ram, prepared for collision. He runs in a round arc to the side of the lunging white guy with terrific speed, but the white guy closes in, throws himself and wraps his arms around the Latin guy's waist, and pulls him down to the ground, the two men rolling over each other. Dust mushrooms around their twisting bodies. Once they come to a stop, both men are laughing, the Latin guy still hugging the ball at his side. The laugh is careless, at ease. Men at play.

The clip ends. This one: two minutes, twelve seconds.

"Let's call the darker one Sergio. He looks like a Sergio."

I sip from my wine glass, a grassy Pinot Grigio from the shop around the corner on Sunset Boulevard. It's become a new ritual: whenever I get sent a clip at work I text Andre, and he prepares the popcorn while I grab the wine on my way home. "What makes him a Sergio?" I ask.

"I don't know. Sergio is like one of those crooners with the big cool-looking mic, like a Humphrey Bogart, like a heartbreaker."

"Then why not call him Humphrey?" I deadpan.

He looks at me with his dark, lashless eyes. I can see the fixed smile, searching for a witty retort, something to carry us along, but Andre's not one to think fast with words, and resorts instead to a smile. He uses his body more to say things. I always know when he folds his arms that he is struggling with a thought not quite resolute, and when he pushes his tongue to the roof of his mouth he is insulted, and when he refuses me in bed, which is often lately, it's because he feels emasculated.

He pulls a piece of paper from his back pocket, opens it up and hands it to me. It's a sales listing of a house in our neighborhood. "Raj at the realty sent me this. It's been on the market for sixteen months. Seller won't reduce, not desperate, lives in New York. It's not going to move."

"So?"

Andre leans in wide-eyed, his tall frame bends like a bow around me. "We could stay there, until it sells, which could be a long time, with this market. Rent-free. We'd be doing them a favor, keeping the place lived-in. We'd only need to work around showings."

"What about this place?" I ask, the attitude pushing out with my lips. I know what I look like: my grandmother when she argued with my mother, which was often, and during family dinners ("Child, I'm not leaving this house for no old folks home"), and out the lips would go, like a wall between mother and daughter, like bumpers to ease a collision. I loved the gesture, even as a little girl—so expressive. I copied it, and now it happens without my even knowing.

Andre stations his large hand on the back of my head, which I want to lean back into, to feel its strength, its comfort, but I don't dare. He kisses the top of my head, whispers, "We could save, until I find a new job. And the house is really nice, right?"

I look at the picture again. It *is* really nice, big, a yard, lots of space, those old craftsmen features—the built-in cabinets, mammoth eaves on the porch—and in the heart of Silver Lake. It's probably nestled into one of the hills, a good view of the glittering lights of Hollywood. My flat doesn't have a view of anything but the garage wall and the sidewalk. But I like my apartment. I chose it. I toss the paper down and it slaps the table a bit too loud. Andre winces.

"Where do you think those guys are? You think they're military?" I ask.

"Afghanistan, maybe Iraq? Who the fuck is filming them is what I want to know."

"Maybe the Mojave," I say.

This football clip is much shorter than the others. Some of them will run ten minutes, even longer. The last one, sent five days before, was a night scene, the same two men sitting around a fire, the glow of their faces a painting in motion, flickering brush strokes, the dark framing their bodies. The white guy was whittling a piece of thin wood with a pocket knife, Sergio picking dirt out of his nails. They were sharing phobias while the fire kept them out of the dark. Sergio: snakes and torture. The white guy: being buried alive. Both: terrified of God. Sergio confesses, "Whenever I see a man tortured in a movie, I cry. I can't help it." The white guy stares into the fire, and says, "I don't cry. I haven't cried since I was kid." The talk is so intimate—maybe childhood friends, or in the same platoon, battalion, whatever you call it. But why were they alone? At least it seemed they were alone—along with the person behind the camera, if there was one. Where were the rest of the guys? Were these guys AWOL, or stranded? Neither made sense—who would have sent me the clips? There's something so erotic about that, sending these clips to me, that only I get to see them. And that by letting Andre see them he would feel the eroticism, too. Or, that's what I hoped.

"Let's call the white guy Dolph. He looks German, or something."

The clips started coming in a little over a month ago. I had been writing reviews for *Cinephiliac*, an online blog for film geeks—real indie, obscure stuff—for three weeks when the first arrived in my mail slot, a jump drive inside a manila envelope, no return address. I came up with this idea that I would review any and all films sent to me, no questions, to drum up interest in my corner of the blog. I blasted it boldly on any and every film chatroom and forum I could find: "No film is turned away. Short films, long films, grad school films, films shot with your GoPro, your smartphone."—and posted my work address to avoid any lurking internet trolls stalking outside my window. I thought it was a great idea, a populist idea, a small effort to democratize the elitist world of art reviews. Much of the submissions were wannabes in LA sending me their undergrad reel. Andre thought it was genius, but he thought most of my ideas were brilliant.

Twenty-five bucks a blog, up to five per week. This was my first professional writing gig, sort of: my nine-to-fiver was as a grant writer for a homeless services center downtown. It was something I felt had purpose, but the work was dry, sometimes painfully technical: assembling statistical data, testimonials, tables of contents, captions to publicity photos. It all became so repetitive, recaps of the same mantras: we do great stuff, we are worth your generosity. Cover pages of little black kids looking up at some white bitch smiling down on them, her hand reaching out as if she were giving the girl the world, and not just a crayon to draw with. *Look at the good we do.*

Some of the submissions for my blog were legit. Beautifully shot art films, funny narrative shorts, a full-length action pic that had to cost some cash to produce. But there was a whole lot of real bad shit, too. Heavy-sigh melodrama, confessional documentaries with overly symbolic shots of clocks and clouds. And the litany of amateur porn was something I hadn't expected. Some of the submissions were so bad I'd post them on the blog just to revel in the fact that someone took the time and energy to make it, thought they had something important to say. It takes all kinds, especially in a city like LA Everyone thinks they're the next big thing, if only they would meet so-and-so, or get an agent, or get their script, their headshot, their reel, their portfolio, in the right hands. I guess I was in that category, too—I wanted to be the next Kenneth Turan or Lucy Lippard—and I thought this blog opp was the first step in getting there, wherever *there* was.

I wouldn't have even had much interest in the Sergio and Dolph clips if it weren't for the first one being so memorable, so *not* film school. No skill in the shot whatsoever. The clip had no edits, and the sound was ambient—there was no boom, no mixing, no soundtrack. Dolph and Sergio were outside, in the washed-out brown dirt of the desert, both wearing fatigues, sweat patches bleeding through their tank tops. They were arguing, though the words were indecipherable because of how far they were from the recorder. A jeep was half in frame in the distance. Dolph was more agitated, flinging his arms in large gestures while walking in circles, the veins on his temple flexing with his open jaw, Sergio following him, also animated, trying to calm Dolph down. They did this for a few minutes, when all of a sudden Dolph turned around and sort of smacked Sergio on the cheek. It wasn't a full-on smack, but more a taunt, *c'mon tough guy*, which shocked Sergio as much as it did me. Sergio raised his hands up in concession, and then Dolph reached forward and smacked him again, this time harder. Sergio backed up, shaking his head, and Dolph advanced, and smacked him even harder. Sergio turned to retreat, but Dolph swung his fist and caught Sergio on the shoulder. Dolph swung again and this time hit Sergio's neck. Sergio peered up at Dolph, clutching what would certainly be a hell of a bruise. His face was so pathetic, his big dark puppy-dog eyes. It was like a deep love of some kind. The clip froze with those eyes looking up at Dolph, so innocent and beautiful that you didn't even notice that Dolph was tilting his head back in a laugh at just the moment before the clip ended. Six minutes, twelve seconds. I remember sitting so still when it ended. Who would send in a clip like this? Did they want it reviewed? It didn't seem like it was a film at all, more like voyeurism, maybe even filming these guys without them knowing. But who would be out in the middle of a desert, with nothing else in the shot but a partial jeepand a shitload of sand and rock?

When I brought it home to show Andre, he thought it was a teaser for a snuff film, "Nothing like a little violence to get people into shit." It sounded so crass at first, but he had a point. It caught *my* attention. I didn't review the clip for the site. There was something so intimate about it—too intimate—and not like the amateur porn, but like it was made only for me, and I wanted to keep it for myself. I can't deny that I got excited when, a few days later, I received another manila envelope delivered to my mail slot. Again, no note, no name, no return address, just a jump drive. I texted Andre, and the tradition began.

Some clips are random, even abstract. One of the first was of them making some kind of stew in a large pot, the pink and purple dusk of the desert sky silhouetting their brawny necks. Sergio pared carrots, Dolph peeled open a can of beans. The camera kept going in and out of focus—maybe a basic cell phone or point-and-shoot video feature—mostly framing their backs as they prepared the meal in silence. They acted like they didn't even know the camera was there. Barely any dialogue. Seven minutes, fifteen seconds. Andre mused that it was a reminder of daily life during wartime. I thought it was more a domestic portrait, an establishing shot to convey the trust in their relationship. Maybe both. Was it a documentary of some kind?

Another clip was of them sniffing each other's armpits. It was daytime, high sun, and obviously hot. The camera was static, as usual, about waist level. The guys were lifting concrete blocks and moving them somewhere out of frame, only to then return. Both had their shirts off, Dolph's tucked into the back of his fatigues, which had a triangle of sweat just above his ass. Instinctually, he wiped his hands on his shirt, then sniffed his naked armpit, the way men do, and pruned his face. Sergio then raised his own arm and tucked his nose into the crook, its dark tuft of hair. He grinned, arm still raised, and nodded to Dolph, who took it as an invitation, and brought his own face into Sergio's armpit. There was a moment, almost sincere, like Dolph was considering the odor like a fine wine, before Sergio laughed, and then Dolph tried to push Sergio's face into his, long dark-blond hairs clumped together from sweat. Four minutes, twenty-seven seconds.

"That's some gay-ass shit right there," Andre said.

"I think they're a couple," I said.

Andre snorted. "Really?"

"Yeah. You don't think so?"

"I don't know. They don't, I mean, they're in the Army, or something. Maybe they're just close, like brothers."

"News flash, boo: there are gay dudes in the military."

"No. I know. They just don't *seem* like gay guys."

My lip curled, and I turned away from him; it wasn't worth sharing my irritation. If I chastised him, he would look at me with a dumbfounded expression, open his hands in front of me, like I was tripping on him. But, still. You would think he'd have experienced enough of that ignorant bullshit in his own life. How many times had he been asked if he played basketball, or had a big dick?

He brings up the house for sale again while eating pancakes at Millie's, the sidewalk patio full of dogs, children, skinny white guys with beards. I say to him, Let's enjoy the sunshine.

He brings it up again when we're driving to a reading, one of my favorite local authors, at Skylight, a bookstore in Los Feliz. I say to him, Let's enjoy the night.

And he brings it up again when we are cuddling up on the couch, watching reruns of *The Sopranos*.

"I just hate that you're paying all the rent. It's not right. I'm trying to help."

I turn off the TV, and lead Andre to the bedroom. I lift his shirt up slowly, to admire the long line of his torso, the lean muscle of his stomach, the thin hairs that circle his navel and chest, his entire body the color of cinnamon. ("I'm a quarter Irish," he claimed the first time

I laid in his arms). I sit him on the bed.

I take his hands and slip them onto my hips, and begin to unbutton. He looks at me curiously, like he's not sure what happens next. I unclasp my bra, and lean towards him, and kiss his neck, lick his ear. I want to cohere the scene. I whisper, "This helps."

He breathes in, "I can't tonight, baby. I'm sorry."

"Why?" I ask.

"I don't know. I just..."

I collapse my head onto his shoulder. We haven't had sex in weeks. Lately, I'm the only one making the effort.

He kisses the top of my head, and something about the sweetness of it, the *nice-ness* of it, ticks me off, and I storm out of the bedroom, into the kitchen, to cool myself down.

I met Andre in the most typical way—a bar—so not the story I want to tell. He approached me with his killer grin, half-empty Manhattan in hand, steady and cool. He didn't open with a lame question or stock come-on. "Hello," he said. I was with two of my friends from work, Kendra and Billy, having a happy hour cocktail. Kendra kicked my calf and muttered, "Holy fuck." Andre was calf-kicking material; in a white button-up as white as his teeth, his face smooth, and that sumptuous color of cinnamon, high cheek bones ("I got some Cherokee in me, too"), tall and sinewy, large dark eyes. There's no doubt he was hot. "Hello," I answered back, already pushing my lips out, attitude for days.

What impressed me was just how at ease the man was, like he didn't have a single issue, a complete rarity in such an anxious place like LA. And how beautiful he was—that was the word. "Don't fuck it up," Kendra advised, and winked. They knew of my recent string of lovers, how I felt none of them were worth more than a few dates. Billy sort of turned his body away from the whole interaction, sulking into his cocktail at the edge of the bar. I knew he wanted to be more than just a colleague by the way he lingered his eyes on me at work. It's always nice to know someone out there wants you. It provides you some leverage. And you never know when that guy you keep on the sidelines will come in handy.

I wasn't looking for anything when I met Andre. I had spent the years after college going from musician to poet to artist, all lasting long enough to be significant, something to write about, but not enough to be a very interesting story. I basically dated Silver Lake, a bunch of skinny white boys. And I wouldn't have even considered Andre if it hadn't been for this abysmal string of failed attempts with said musicians, poets, and artists. I thought I should be with someone creative, together staying up into the late hours discussing process, critiquing each other's work, erupting in temperamental bouts of claws-out fighting, having equally eruptive make-up sex. Robert Mapplethorpe and Patti Smith. Beyoncé and Jay-Z. This was how I imagined my love life to be, but it was mostly just the fighting. I grew tired of it after a while, and went on hiatus, exhausted by the attention it took away from my writing.

That's why Andre was so refreshing when I met him. He wasn't creative in the slightest—a real estate agent, apparently really good at it. I had no interest whatsoever in his line of work, but he discussed it with a passion equal to an artist's. He thought it was philanthropy, helping newlyweds, young families, empty nesters realize their dreams, transition to the next phase of their life. He saw owning a house as the measure of success and happiness. I couldn't have cared less about home-ownership, but I admired his conviction. He had just started saving for his own, and I thought maybe I'd been going about dating all wrong—if I was with someone financially solid, I could write all the time; instead of another artist, always broke and needy, I needed to be with a patron.

Andre would come home from work fully satisfied with a sale he made, his bright-colored shirts crisp and well fitted, talking about the couple as if he had known them for years, bouncing around the kitchen of my apartment—later to be his apartment, too—searching for potato chips and beer, talking loudly about the transaction, his body full of purpose and confidence. It was so sexy, to be sure of oneself without even a hint of arrogance. None of the scrawny white-boy artists had any confidence, always searching for affirmation ("What do you think of this? It's terrible, isn't it?") Andre didn't need affirmation. That is, until the housing crisis blew up and he lost his job. He started to bum around during the day in his pajamas, searching job posts, watching TV. Despite the rough tumble the industry had taken, he didn't search for any kind of work besides real estate. ("This is what I was meant to do").

The first couple months after he lost his job, it was kind of nice having him around when I got home from work. He was a decent cook, and when I walked in the door, the apartment smelled like cayenne or rosemary. He grew up in Los Angeles, and made his dishes green and spicy. My family, all from Houston, complained about California food, whenever they visited. "It's too frou-frou," my sister Alexis always said. "Where's the butter?"

By the third month, the apartment began to feel small. Andre was pulling unemployment, but I was the breadwinner. It wasn't how I saw myself at twenty-six, and when we fought, I'd share that with him. He began disappearing for hours on end, sometimes coming home well after me, in sweat pants, the sky dark against the Hollywood Hills. When I'd ask where he was, he'd say, "Just getting some air" or "Around the neighborhood." He could have been doing anything: getting drunk, fucking some prissy blond bitch, selling his ass for mattress money. But, you know what? I wasn't upset. I didn't feel much of anything, and eventually I stopped asking where he was.

We are on the couch watching TV. I am dozing in and out on Andre's chest, thinking of work, dreaming a little of Houston—something I don't often do. I'm remembering my life there in that slow, provincial city, that urge to flee after I graduated college, that urge to live in a place with culture with a capital 'C.' That's why I bolted to LA as soon as I finished college. I did miss the warm, balmy nights, though.

"What kind of story do you think it's going to be?" Andre's voice sounds like it is coming from inside his chest, deep and muffled. He is stroking my hair. "You know, Sergio and Dolph?"

"Not sure. Maybe it's not a narrative," I mumble.

"It seems like it is. What do you think it's trying to say?"

I had thought about this many times, even after watching the second and third clips. There were some common elements: the men, the desert, a certain quietness. Who would send these clips, if not the guys themselves? And if so, why? Was it *cinéma vérité*? I don't feel like I can have a real conversation about it with Andre. I am too tired to explain what *cinéma vérité* is, anyway.

"Maybe it's not trying to say anything," I say.

"Can something ever not say anything?"

"It's more complicated than that," I sigh, and drop deeper into the doze again, hearing the rise and fall of Andre's chest, and am too sleepy to wonder why he has stopped stroking my hair.

Another manila envelope comes in the midst of a busy day. I am finishing up a brand-new grant proposal when the intern drops it on my desk. I want to rip it open right then, give myself distraction. Instead, I text Andre. He replies, *I'll get the popcorn going!*

Andre is in his pajamas again when I arrive home. "You really need to wash those," I say. He grins, kisses me on the neck. "I made some tacos. But first, popcorn," and disappears into the kitchen. I pull out my laptop, open the manila envelope, and load the jump drive, as Andre slides back onto the couch.

Sergio is laying shirtless on the jeep's hood, his arms raised, hands behind his head. He has a broad chest, hairless, with tiny dark brown nipples. His pant-legs are rolled up, and he is barefoot. Even his feet look strong. The sun is beaming directly on him, his eyes slightly squinting. He is visibly sweating, and it trickles down the side of his face, his neck, the slope of his chest muscles, along his sides. The camera is steady, steadily resting on Sergio laying against the hood, almost vulnerable. He doesn't acknowledge the camera. Does he even know it's there, or is he intentionally *not* looking at it? Both possibilities make me hot. I see a tattoo I hadn't noticed before, a small gecko stretched along his ribs, the head facing downward, like it is running toward safety in the presumed shelter of his fatigues. His hands lower to his chest, as if he is going to wipe off the sweat, fingers splayed, moving slowly. Slowly, he circles his nipples, almost absently. He slides his hands along his chest, its rounds and mounds, across his stomach and, gently, yet with no hesitation, they disappear into the front of his fatigues. He arches his neck up, lightly parts his lips, his chest rising with him, eyes closed.

The clip ends. One minute twenty-three seconds. I feel the incredible silence after the screen goes black.

Some seconds later I realize Andre is looking at me with a big grin.

"What?" I ask.

He laughs, a far off sound that could have come from another room.

I ask, "Where was Dolph?"

"Behind the camera?"

"Why *this* time?"

"See. Maybe they *are* gay for each other," he says.

"I don't know. Maybe Dolph wasn't there."

"Then who shot this?"

"I don't know. The mysterious camerawoman?"

"Maybe Sergio. I mean, it was kind of…"

"Indulgent?"

"Yeah. Like a selfie you would send to someone you liked," he muses.

"I think it goes deeper than that."

Andre is looking intently at me again, his grin fixed.

"What?" I ask again.

His eyes drop a bit. "Nothing," he says.

I lightly punch him on the shoulder. He shakes his head.

"You think Sergio is good looking," he says.

"Why you say that?" I ask.

"I saw you. You were into that." He nods at the laptop.

"What are you talking about?"

Andre keeps grinning, but his eyes look a little distant. I quickly close the laptop and rise from the table.

"Hey," he says. "Have you thought any more about the house?"

"No, I've been too busy," I say. Actually, I had thought about it, but every time I imagined moving into the place, with Andre, I felt like I was walking on the thin ledge of a steep hillside. "I'm going to take a bath. It was so hot today in the office. I feel gross."

I walk into the hallway to the bathroom, and before I close the door I hear Andre say, weakly, "Okay."

Andre becomes obsessed with Dolph and Sergio after the clip on the car hood. Even on evenings when there isn't a clip, he starts in on his theories about their purpose. He sits further from me on the couch. He is convinced now that there is no cameraperson, that they are living off the grid, or that they aren't out of the closet to their friends and family, that they met in the military, and somehow are channeling their closeted love affair into this kind of exhibitionism—my word, not his. And on days that I do get a clip, he writes down the events of the sequence, like he is cataloging evidence, in hopes of unearthing the master plan for all of these segments. I have received twelve at this point. Almost three months since the first clip. Almost four months since Andre lost his job.

"It's like an engine," he says. "You have to figure how to make sense of all the little pieces to know the whole thing."

"Like the anatomy of a relationship," I say.

"Yeah," he says, that distant grin again.

When the next clip comes—same manila envelope, no return address—I don't text Andre about it right away. I'm not sure why, exactly, but I am aware of a kind of pleasure in possibly keeping it from him. I shake the feeling away, and pull out my phone.

I got another one, I text.

When I arrive home, Andre is once again in his pajamas, laying on the couch watching a rerun of *South Park*. He hasn't shaved in a several days, and his beard is beginning to cover up his lips. He gets up, leans in to kiss me. He has lost weight. "Have you even brushed your teeth today," I ask.

He retracts, looking apologetic to the floor, "Of course."

"Popcorn?" I ask.

"You want some?"

I slide the bottle of wine onto the coffee table and pull out my laptop, load the jump drive.

The shot is very out of focus, and the camera is pointing directly at the sun, making it difficult to discern what appears to be a single figure in the distance.

"Is that Sergio?" Andre asks, squinting into the computer screen.

"I think so," I say.

At first the figure looks like it is walking away from the camera, but soon we realize he is running, the ripple of hot air against desert floor warping his image. The rest of the shot is wide-open sand and rock desert, chocolate-colored hills way out on the horizon, the sky a cloudless pale blue. There is no sign of the jeep, or Dolph.

A few seconds later, there is a very loud crack, too much sound for the recorder, which makes the ring distorted. Immediately after, the figure disappears.

I sit up quickly. "What was that?"

"Was that a gunshot?"

"I think so. I think Sergio just got shot!"

"Play it again," he says, and leans in closer to the laptop. I click the arrow, and the same blown out scene, the pale ground, the same loud distorted invasion of sound, the same watery distant figure there, and then not there.

"Holy shit. Do you think that was real?" I ask.

"Again," Andre says. He is intent on the screen, his head pulled forward. It's certainly Andre, the open brow, the rounded tip of nose, the softness of his full lips, but his eyes are something else. They have a wildness to them, or a hunger, but not quite like desire. I don't know. If eyes could seethe, it would be more like that. It's a totally new look. I thought I had seen every look he could possibly have; he didn't have that many, really. I could almost predict his faces, they had all become so familiar. And now this face. I am not sure what it is, what it tells me.

"Are you going to play it?" he asks, his chin, jawline and cheekbones rendered severe by the light from the laptop's screen.

I don't know who he is right now, and for once I don't know what to say, so I quietly hit replay.

The clips keep coming, but now only Dolph is present in them—no Sergio. The very next clip—four minutes, eighteen seconds—is of Dolph making dinner, slicing onions into a small frying pan, the sizzle of the vegetables as they hit the hot metal. And nothing else. My stomach turns as I watch it. Andre asks to replay, but this time he immediately takes the laptop from my control, and plays the clip in extreme slow motion, examining each frame as if it holds a clue to the disappearance of Sergio, that look again on his face, that seething look. I can't deal with it, or the possibility that Sergio has been hurt, or something worse.

I tell Andre we should call the police, but imagine aloud how the police would respond. *Lady, you are reporting a possible murder that is entirely based on video clips being sent to you, possibly fictional narrative, possibly not happening any time recently? This is LA, lady. We have real problems to deal with.* Andre doesn't respond, not even a grunt or a subtle raising of his eyebrows to acknowledge that he's heard me, clicking away on the computer, staring at the next frame, and the next frame.

I retreat to the bedroom. I'm tired.

"Why is the story still going?" Andre asks over breakfast the following Saturday morning. We have received two more clips, both starring only Dolph. The frequency of the clips following Sergio's disappearance unnerves me, and my hands shake when I think about it. A few times when I'm alone I well up with tears just thinking about him being dead. I don't even know this guy, but I cry for him; I haven't cried in years, since I was a child.

One clip is of Dolph climbing up a rock face in the scorching heat of the desert. The camera is static, as usual, a long shot. The desert landscape stretches on both sides of the rise, variations of brown and tan, the pale, almost white sky blending into the sun-bleached hills far beyond where Dolph climbs, his shirt wrapped around his head, the muscles of his arms and back pushing out with each clasp of rock, with each effort to pull the rest of his large body. Twelve minutes, eight seconds.

The second clip is a medium shot of Dolph at night, sitting in front of a campfire, pushing the wood coals around with a stick, little pieces of fire rising and dancing around in the air with each disturbance. Is this maybe another part of the same sequence we've seen with the two of them, Sergio and Dolph, the campfire? It's impossible to know. He softly sings, something out of tune, but familiar all the same, a military song that I've heard in a film, perhaps. He sings this to himself, his eyes lowered, and I feel that Dolph is mourning. Is he lonely? Is he lamenting the death of Sergio? If Dolph shot Sergio, is he lamenting his actions? I don't share these questions with Andre, and we watch in silence. The more I think about the clips, and the more they keep coming, the more I am disturbed by their continuance, and the more Andre leans closer to the computer screen. Wasn't this story about the two of them, about their existence together in the desert? Or, was everything that came before Sergio's disappearance the first act of a different story, that all the shots with Sergio were establishing scenes for us to feel the loss when it came? That the real story is about Dolph, coming to terms with his lover's death? With being alone, forever?

Andre rises from the couch. "I'm going out. I'll see you later." He grabs his keys, his jacket, and within seconds has already closed the door behind him.

I collect all the flash drives together, number them in the order they were received, and put them in an old pencil box I've had since seventh grade, pictures of Britney Spears grinning with coquettish poses in a Catholic school uniform. I think I will turn the drives in to the police, soon.

Andre returns home just before I wake to go to work. The morning is barely coming into the window, that cool cornflower light.

At work, during a too-long lunch break, I watch all the clips, one after the other, the quiet shots of the desert, the intimate moments of men at play, the night shots around the fire, the scenes of labor without context. There is no camerawoman. Every shot indeed is static. The camera is still, recording without comment, documenting without bias, solely a blank objective stare, like the eyes of a shark. When I get to the clip of Sergio on the hood of the jeep, sweating on himself, against the metal, his smooth brown hand sliding along the skin of his sturdy chest as his lips part, the fluid motion of his fingers slipping under the waistband of his fatigues, and the elegant arching of his back, I am overcome with that soft heat inside me that starts low in my belly and then shoots out all along my limbs. Something about seeing this image again, now knowing he might be dead, makes it feel even more intimate. No one will see him do this ever again, maybe his last time, and I get to see him in this moment, this full enjoyment of himself. I get wet right then and there, sitting at my desk at work, feel it cling to the thin fabric of my underwear.

I walk over to Billy's office and ask him if he wants to get a drink with me after work. I add *alone*, and tongue my lips just enough, so he understands, and then return to my desk.

I open the front door to my apartment, and there is Andre. He is splayed out on the armchair, shirtless, wearing fatigues and boots. His arms are raised and rested behind his head, long sinewy torso further defined by his flexing. He pretends he hadn't heard the door, eyes closed. He lowers his arms and begins circling his nipples with his finger. I watch him for a minute, curious, but as he slides his hand down his body, towards his dick, fury surges up from my gut and into my temples.

"What the fuck?" I yell, and throw my purse on the couch. I still can smell Billy on my hands, even though I showered at his place.

Andre jars, eyes big as quarters. "What?"

"Really? This is tacky," I say. And then add, "even for you."

"I didn't…what do you mean?"

"The guy is dead, Andre."

"You don't know that."

"He's dead!" I waltz into the kitchen, get some water, try to put as much space between him and me as I can. I drink fast and loud and angry. I can feel the water getting hot against my lips. He follows me.

"This is what you want, isn't it?"

"What?"

He splays his hands around, then points to the fatigues. "This."

"What the fuck are you talking about?"

"It's not me, right? It was never me, *right*?"

I push my lips out, sway my head, and try to steady and deadpan my voice, to shoot him down. "There's always someone." I go to the bedroom and close the door behind me.

Inside the room, I want to break things. I want to slide the contents off the dresser in one clean sweep, like you see in the movies. I want to put fabric in my mouth and rip it, destroy something. Instead, I stand in the middle of the room clenching my fists, replaying Andre's pathetic mimicry. There's something so desperate about him, laying there waiting for me to return home. He even bought fatigues. How could he have possibly thought that I would enjoy that? And, that's when it comes to me: maybe it wasn't meant to be enjoyed.

Andre's voice comes from beyond the bedroom door. "I'll see you later," he says, calmly. A few moments after, the front door squeaks open and closes, and the apartment takes on a noticeable silence.

Almost a month goes by before I receive another clip, the last. It arrives the same way—manila envelope, no return address, a jump drive. I betray a gasp at the sight of the familiar handwriting. But I don't wait until I'm home to watch it this time. Andre moved into the house for sale, and we haven't spoken in weeks. He gathered his belongings while I was at work, and dropped the key in the mail slot. There was no note, no long text message or voicemail. It was the cleanest breakup I ever had. He left with the same effortlessness that brought him to me in that bar two years ago. It's like he never existed.

I look around the office. Everyone is on calls, in meetings, paying no attention to me, but I still lean in close to block what is playing on the monitor screen. I can barely get the jump drive in, my hands shaking.

The final clip is long, twenty-two minutes, three seconds. Both Sergio and Dolph are sitting in front of the fire. I wonder if this is indeed part of the same scene in the past clip, broken up for effect, since both men are positioned in the exact same spot, the camera still, steady, and now somehow menacing.

Dolph is asking Sergio questions, almost interview style. When was your first kiss? When did you lose your virginity? How do you know when someone is in love? With all of them, Sergio sheepishly grins, looks down to the ground. His answers are generic, not at all interesting. They blend into the dark night. I am more interested in the way the light warms their faces, the smooth slope of Sergio's jawline, the rugged angles of Dolph. I watch this like a dance, allowing myself to enjoy the shapes, the color, the composition of their intimacy. And words float into the night, indistinct, and I enjoy the timbre of their voices—Dolph's flat, deep and gravelly like the desert floor, Sergio's clean and clear like the desert sky. My eyes slowly lose focus, and the blur of the computer screen is equally beautiful, its indistinguishable senses.

Sergio's laugh stirs me from this aesthetic trance. It is a full, easy laugh, and he rocks his whole upper body back, briefly disappearing from the firelight and into the desert dark, and then returns, rubs his neck.

Dolph says, "So, what have you learned from all of it?"

I wonder what he implies. I guess I will play this clip back later to discover what "all of it" means.

Sergio grins, one last time, looks at Dolph with a squint in his eyes, like a secret passing between them. He wipes his hands along the lap of his fatigues, and stands, looks straight into the fire, a grin on his face, sweet and somehow distant. "Men need to be loved so much."

The clip goes black. There are no credits, there is no acknowledgement that this is the end. Just blackness. I sit there for a moment, waiting for something in me to feel a sense of resolve, for there to be the catharsis gleaned from scene, for there to be an end to the beginning and the middle, but there is only the ringing phones in the office, the faint smell of burnt coffee, the sterile glow of the computer screen.

SAVING A BIRD

Walking home with Michael from an engagement brunch at Max and Carol's flat, Colin saw the bird. He was drunk on mimosas, his feet clomping the sidewalk erratically, watching the neighborhood slightly blur as he ambled. He knew he drank too much at the brunch, knew that he was getting a tad sloppy, but pretended not to see Michael's occasional furrowed glance from across the room while he chatted with all the familiar faces, talking of new restaurants that opened in the neighborhood, cooing over Carol's engagement ring, them asking Colin when he and Michael would "get hitched, now that it was legal." The high-pitched clucks and tuts and the doe-eyed sentiments and pats on the shoulder tightened Colin's chest, and he gulped down a glass whenever he felt the urge to run out of the crowded shotgun apartment, down the narrow stairs, to catch his breath. It was a relief when the brunch began to break up; Colin looked forward to the walk home.

They were nearing their side of the neighborhood when Colin suddenly blocked Michael's chest with his arm. "Wait," he said. "Look."

"What?" Michael squinted forward, scanning the intersection—the blue-black asphalt, the telephone pole with stapled announcements of dance shows, punk shows, art shows, the Italianate rowhouses painted gray, purple, olive green, faded by the wet air, the coffee shop across the street, the steep hill rising into the verdant mound of Buena Vista Park. "What?"

"Look," Colin said, and pointed. He lowered himself down, about two feet from a baby pigeon, perched in the crosswalk of the street, about a foot from the curb. The bird was still, save miniscule twitches of its head. "It's alive."

Michael didn't lower himself down, but saw the bird. He scratched his nose, and looked around.

"It looks stunned," Colin said. "Maybe it fell out of the nest. It doesn't look hurt."

"It'll get hurt, sitting out there. The cars," Michael said, looking at Colin, then back around.

"The people. It's on the cross-walk."

"Poor guy. I wonder what happened?"

"Go into the market, and get a box," Colin said. He lowered his body more, trying to see if there was injury.

"For the bird?"

"Maybe it's scared."

"Colin, get up. You look silly."

"We have to save it."

"And what are we going to do with a bird? It's probably diseased, or something."

"Michael, please," Colin said.

Michael shrugged, "All right," and turned toward the market.

Colin leaned a little closer to the baby pigeon, which didn't seem to notice him. It lay still, tucked into itself, no flutter of movement. Colin never recalled seeing a bird so motionless, and he even thought to touch it to see if it responded. But he stopped himself, afraid that the bird would scare and possibly run into road. It seemed the bird couldn't fly—why else would it be sitting in the road? He searched in his mind for any information he had about birds, recalling poorly produced nature programs on Sunday afternoon TV, or those narrated by Richard Attenborough on the mating and hunting habits of species he'd never heard of, or his high school science class. All he could conjure was some nesting details on American birds of prey, and that ravens and crows were the same thing, and nothing else.

Colin was grateful. Not for the bird, per se, but for the urgency of the moment. Despite feeling vague with all the champagne in his gut, he never could shake the tightness around his chest, which came over him more and more these days, and this bird required attention, and had nothing to do with the engagement, and the questions it conjured with his own relationship. *When are you and Michael going to be hitched?*

Carol and Max had been together for almost as long as Colin and Michael. Carol was a life-long San Franciscan, born and raised in the Outer Sunset, which made her all the more rare to their friends, who mostly came from Southern California via almost everywhere else. Max had been a colleague of Michael's back in Los Angeles, at the same film studio where Colin and Michael had met. Colin was working as a production assistant, which meant he was basically a coffee-fetcher, an errand-boy. Michael was the director of photography. He saw things within a frame, one that he constructed, lines that made a box. He loved to assemble the perfect shot, from the studio to the living room to the bedroom to the bed. "Stop," he would say, he and Colin walking through Buena Vista Park where the dense stand of trees opened just enough to see the Bridge drop into the Marin Headlands; "Stop," he would say, Colin laying on his side naked, legs bent softly against the dark brown comforter after making love. Colin used to think it charming, this love, this need to seize beauty. After so many years together, though, the charm had worn down to, at once, an affection and an annoyance, and Colin would roll his eyes. "Does everything need to be captured, Michael?"

"We are hunters," Michael would say, his dark eyes smiling.

Twelve hours after they had been formally introduced on set, Colin slept with Michael. Colin had been ordered to get Starbucks for the crew, and when he delivered the rounds, Michael later said he'd immediately been stunned by Colin's pure royal blue eyes and his rich red lips, set within a face where skin and facial hair were the exact same golden-peach. Though he wasn't traditionally a good-looking man, kind of short and slightly pear-shaped, enough people had been intensely struck by the colors in Colin's doughy face to make him think he perhaps had a future as an actor; he had a *look*. Michael made sure to touch Colin's fingers when he passed over the Venti soy latte, no foam, and used his authority and lowered eyelashes to create a picture of something dark and inviting. Michael made it a priority to get what he wanted, and Colin easily leaned with suggestion. The sheer solid, resolved desire in Michael's face felt like gravity to Colin—*this man has no doubt*—and his stomach tingled. Anyone would have seen Michael's erect stance, his head looming over Colin's tilted head, grinning, their fingers touching, and easily predicted the evening.

What Michael hadn't known then was that Colin was dating someone else: Rio, a fellow actor he had met on the set of another film, another PA job. For almost two years, Colin and Rio had been having sex, dancing in the West Hollywood clubs, ending up in Sunset Strip hotels doing blow off of twink magazines, or passing out on strangers' couches. Colin had thought it was all a sort of research for growing up, or living, something that could not be done back in Oklahoma. He didn't love the nights in WeHo, but he liked the romantic aesthetic enough, the grimy indie-film narrative—blurred lights, close-up impressions of hands and flesh and teeth, underwater laughter, the beauty of people so different than himself—and he felt that it was a rite of passage into cynicism, which he had naively confused with California worldliness.

Colin most looked forward to when they would visit Rio's family in Lakewood, where cousins and uncles and grandmothers all lived on the same street, even tore the fences down between houses so the kids could play on the whole block. They would visit for Easter, or a birthday, and as they entered one of the houses – his sister's maybe – Rio would grab Colin's hand instinctively, and pull him into the throng of kissing cheeks, tousling hair, hugs. Colin would return the hugs, making sure to give his whole body to it. They would together make tamales for a holiday, a birthday, Colin fumbling with the masa, trying to spread it too carefully, ripping apart the corn husks. Rio's Tia Espie would laugh and grab Colin's shoulders, and shake. "It's a good thing you're cute, eh Rio?" and wink at her nephew. Colin would drop his eyes in feigned shame and smile, and touch Rio's hand underneath the table. This was when he felt for Rio most – or, rather, didn't feel as much doubt with him, the wildness of their affair - when they were with Rio's family. Not even a gasp the first time Rio brought Colin around. Colin craved that, wished those days more often, wished he could bring a boy home to his parents, but that would never happen.

Not that his family was anything but loving. His parents called him every Sunday after church and his mother still kissed into the phone and his father still told her to stop crying when they were about to hang up, maybe aware that Colin was sometimes crying, too, on the other end. But, they lived out, beyond the suburbs of Tulsa, and they weren't much for surprises, and Colin believed it would hurt them to come out, didn't want to challenge the values that their religion and rural upbringing had hardened into them like Oklahoma clay. They would question what they did wrong, how they failed, and Colin never wanted them to feel that way. If anything, he felt like he could never thank them enough, for the comfort, the bundled safety of the childhood they had created for him and his siblings. He trusted that time would eventually give them the news, the way wrinkles come into a face.

And, not like he would have ever introduced Rio to his parents. Rio wasn't exactly someone who wanted to settle down in a family way. He went out almost every night, loved dressing in tight jeans and t-shirts that easily slid up his shaved stomach, loved playing peek-a-boo across dimly lit bars and laughing louder than he needed to have the glinting eyes of lust gleam on his face. But Rio was fun, and Colin felt like he needed a little Rio to feel more confident about living in LA, about pursuing acting as a career, listening to casting agents say his pictures looked too fat, too fleshy, too Oklahoma – he developed a habit of pulling his shirt away from his flabby middle - about being in such an unstable place, one that always felt like it shook, like it never had a moment of stillness. Colin would sometimes walk along Sunset or Vine or La Brea or Highland, and think he felt the sidewalk trembling, the shouts, the cars, all the sounds competing for space, and none of it directed toward him or aware of him at all. And though he got away from Oklahoma for all that he couldn't be, he missed the closeness of the world there, the coziness of his family, the tight fit of his previous life.

Michael was a little older, Michael was successful, Michael was solid. He knew what he wanted, a rare quality in Los Angeles. There was routine early on with them: Thursday night dinner, the first day of the week that Michael would let himself out because he liked to stay focused at work; gym Monday-Wednesday-Friday morning; a visit with Michael's sister in Ventura once a month, the only family he still talked to or talked about regularly, his parents both dead. Michael's choices were careful. He would Yelp a restaurant before going, compared purchases, debated plans, for the sake of certainty. His catchphrase was "Let me sit on that for a bit." Colin felt warm, swaddled against Michael's tree trunk of a life.

Rio was impulsive, which sometimes created evenings of magic, serendipitous fun, and then other times would make Colin feel dizzy, like he needed to close a door in a small room and lie down. Rio once convinced him to go to an entertainment lawyer's party, "Greg Arakki's gonna be there!" Colin was tired, it was already midnight when Rio stumbled to his apartment from the bar, but Rio begged, and so they dolled themselves up and headed to Hancock Park. The house was a giant pseudo-Tudor the lawyer had just bought. Much of the house was empty, but the dining room table was full of pink, blue and white pills of various shapes that young fashionistas, baby-faced girl-boys, and older industry trolls picked up and ate with the ease of trail mix. "Here," Rio said, and shoved one in Colin's mouth. "Swallow." When Colin woke up the next afternoon naked in a pile of legs and arms, and felt the stickiness around his asshole, and saw Rio laying on top of the entertainment lawyer's salt-and-pepper chest hair, Colin felt like he was being propped on an altar for sacrifice, supported only by a pillar lodged in the small of his back, limbs akimbo and uncontrolled, and the cold in his gut like the one he used to feel as a child – uncertain about a punishment when he disobeyed his parents - rose up higher in him than it ever had, up into his temple, even made him vomit in the lawyer's brand new oversized Travertine sink.

That was his sign, his chunky insides splattered on the limestone. And that is why he chose Michael, so long ago.

And where was Michael? Colin didn't want to pick up the bird with his hands. What if the bird, frightened, ran off straight into traffic, got squashed by a car? What if he crushed the bird by accident? What if? He remembered that some animals are rejected by their mothers if they smell of human flesh, and he hoped he could avoid all that, and just get the bird to safety. He needed a box. What else, he didn't know.

The bird did not move, even as Colin scooted closer to it, scraping the ass of his jeans against the sidewalk. He wanted to see the black beads of its eyes, to get the story of this bird, to figure why it rested in such a precarious place, why it didn't move to safety, at least to the curb. But, the eyes were black beads, deeply set in the ratty feathered head, unblinking. Perhaps this stillness was an instinct in birds, when they know they've made an unanticipated mistake. Colin imagined the bird, moments ago, being too bold, thinking it ready to leave the nest perhaps, opening its not-yet-ready wings on the edge of the twig and string, feeling no connection with the ground below, only to drop like a stone. Or, maybe it had no choice. Maybe the nest was too small, or there wasn't enough food for all the chicks. How terrifying that fall must have been, Colin thought, that leap before the knowing. He kept scooting towards the bird slowly, and noticed the markings of the bird's head, little streaks of white, and imagined how they would probably grow more and more ugly, until it became the thing it would become, a rat with wings.

Colin and Michael's flat in Duboce Triangle was lovely—a terrific word for it, lovely—a generous combination of Michael's impeccable framing and Colin's need for comfort, a little bit of his Oklahoma home, with its soft throw rugs and deep-colored chenille blankets draping over the sofa. They bought the flat a few years ago, when some of Michael's previous TV work went into syndication and Colin had passed the Jurisprudence Exam for Pharmacists. When they hosted dinner parties, they served in a combination of Royal Copenhagen and antique pieces from thrift stores in the Haight, on the large country island of reclaimed oak they had custom-built, yellow curtains, white-painted wood, pillows softening every nook and chair. The décor felt like an accomplishment for Colin, a successful way to carve himself into a shared life with Michael. Michael gave Colin the silent treatment if he bought something without *discussing it*, so Colin learned early on to present his decorating interests in public, so that he could ensure a bit of warmth in the house that, if all Michael, would look like a spread in a Sans Pareil catalog. "You're so silly, with all your hippie crap," Michael would say, and touch Colin's nose. The audience would coo. Colin would tilt his head back in chuckle, playing along, but sometimes imagined sinking his teeth into Michael's furry Italian finger. *Crap?* Michael always had to present his judgments. But Michael would concede with an exaggerated sigh, a shoulder shrug, and a dreamy grin that would give Colin comfort in the knowing that Michael loved him.

They made dinner together at these parties, slinking around one another with ease, Michael touching the small of Colin's back and bringing a ladle to his lips, "taste this" and Colin kissing him, "needs more saffron" and Max and Carol, or some other couple, all in the liquid heavy of wine, cooed with the certainty of their romantic future. They indeed were an attractive couple in this way, Colin thought, intuitive and trusting. Carol always exclaimed, as if it were the first time, "Seriously, though, you boys are lucky, so lucky." Michael gladly accepted the praise, while Colin wiped his hands on his apron and turned away from the arrogance. Sometimes, he imagined pulling Carol into the hallway and whispering his fantasies of leaving Michael, of packing in the middle of the night and slipping into a grungy Greyhound bus seat to Portland, or Utah, or anyplace where the sky was big and the air was clean.

But, Colin knew he was lucky. Who knows where he'd be without Michael? Perhaps still going to auditions for commercials for products he never heard of, using his honey-colored face to sell hand-held appliances or convenience store cookies, never getting a callback, feeling worse about himself, his body, going back to more PA work until the next gig and the next gig, hanging out with men who worked him until the next gig and the next gig. It wasn't so much the meager money as the instability of that life that made him feel exposed and scared. Many times in Los Angeles—walking along the street, the nights with Rio, on his way to an audition—Colin felt like he was in this wide expanse with no edge, that a wind could blow by at any moment and take him off the ground, into an unknown. He longed for a small, tight spot, a tornado shelter, something he could burrow into, cling on, whenever that feeling came over him. Michael would hold Colin for hours on the couch, their bodies fitting together with what seemed to Colin like fate, and Colin would nuzzle his face into Michael's neck, and breathe in the warmth of him, and exhale his gratitude.

One evening soon after Colin had first moved into Michael's West Hollywood apartment, after they had made dinner and were nestling into the couch, Michael took a lock of Colin's hair between his fingers. "Don't go into work tomorrow."

Colin grinned, "Michael! You don't play hooky. Why, what you have in mind?"

"No," Michael said. "I mean, ever. Don't go back."

Colin snorted. He was once again doing PA work for a cable channel recently bought by an even larger cable channel, mostly grabbing lunches and delivering messages to the talent. "And do what?"

"I don't know. What do you want to do?"

Colin sipped his wine, tilted his head, "Well," and blanked. He was surprised how much he had not thought about that, exactly. He wanted to be defiant and say, "I want to be an actor, you ass," but he knew that wasn't really true anymore, and maybe was never true. He sighed at his inability to even know what he wanted. He had gone to college, a small liberal arts school in Oklahoma, not really the most focused experience, experimenting in many things but not serious about any of them. He loved the theatre, and was considered a good character actor, with his animated face, so he chose the major more out of being *some*thing than being *the* thing. But now, after three years in LA and not even scoring a cameo, he stared into his wine glass and began to feel that cold in the gut again.

"Hey," Michael said. "I'm only asking."

"I like to help people," Colin said, still gazing into the deep berry of the Cabernet.

"How about you go back to school for something? Think about it. I'm making enough, you can focus, you don't have to worry about money, and then do something respectable."

"But what?" Colin asked.

"Don't make a decision yet. I just want you to be happy."

Colin didn't know he was unhappy, but the way Michael had said it so matter-of-factly, so open-faced, he wondered. Michael had that way of seeming so sure, and it made Colin doubt his own assurances. Maybe he didn't think carefully enough about his own choices, the way Michael did. He certainly never felt that confident about them. He would waffle with the slightest argument or suggestion. Maybe this career change was the next phase in growing up.

He eventually chose medical school. It felt important, not like acting, something more altruistic. He walked around their apartment, "I care about people, right? It makes sense to do something where I help people, you think?" Michael approved, cupped Colin's head with his hands, "such a good choice," and followed through with his promise and, if anything, with more generosity than Colin could have predicted, never a complaint, never a "I pay all this money, and you…" Colin tilted his head, thinking *here is a good man, a man who loves and supports, a good lover, who wants me to be a better version of myself.* If only he could introduce Michael to his parents, they would approve. The one choice they would think was a sensible one was the one he couldn't share. Colin focused, worked harder than he ever had, and did well. He owed that to Michael. And, after he completed his studies, which were neither that difficult or particularly interesting to Colin, it was a job offer at a pharmacy that moved them up to San Francisco. Colin grew giddy over the offer, thinking San Francisco more romantic, and closer to the wild natural California he imagined as a kid. Michael, now a sought-after freelancer, was willing. He put Colin's hair between his fingers and pulled it to the side. "Whatever you want. I never liked LA, anyway."

Just as Colin believed that he might reach his hand out to touch and comfort the baby pigeon, he saw a tall, bearded man with large feet, wearing very large hiking boots, lumber across the crosswalk toward them, looking upwards toward the sky, headphones in his ears, his hands drumming the air. Panic filled Colin, came in through his legs. He immediately imagined the man unknowingly stepping on the bird, squashing the little thing with his oafish mass, the point of contact with soft body and unknowing sole a tragic moment. The man was coming straight towards the bird, his stride heavy, the sound of his boots absorbed by rubber and the noise of the neighborhood, yet Colin could hear the doom-doom-doom. The bird sat there, still, seemingly indifferent to the world around it. What was this bird doing? Was it so paralyzed by the new surroundings that no instinct came to mind? Colin thought it so strange, that nature could be so immobile. It made him sort of angry, and he noticed he was sweating through his shirt, even on this chilly afternoon. Did this bird not get it? The man was coming closer, gigantic to Colin from his perspective on the sidewalk. Colin felt the threat, as if he could predict exactly where the man's feet would land. Was this instinct, too? He wanted to cry out, to stop the man, tell him to stop, but only his face made the protest, a wide-eyed open-mouthed fear that the man didn't even notice, not even with Colin's royal blue eyes wide and electric. Colin needed to scoop the bird, protect it, but he doubted his own ability to do so. What if he injured the chick by picking it up? What if the bird hopped out of his hand and into more danger? The boots kept coming and Colin kept silent and the bird kept still.

Finally, "The bird!" was all Colin could force out, a puff of air through a great wall of worry, but it was much too late, after the man had already lifted up his very large leg and sent it soaring through the air. Gravity now brought it back down to Earth, and right where the baby pigeon had been.

"The bird!" Colin shouted again, and the man, aware that his foot did not meet the normal gravelly macadam, retracted his leg, to reveal the bird, now moving, convulsing, opening and closing its beak furiously. Colin could see the pain in the bird, but it made no sound, just the repetition of its beak, opening and closing, opening and closing.

"You stepped on it!" Colin screamed at the man, who, alarmed, took the headphones off his ears. "You stepped on it!" Now, Colin was crying, surprised by the hot tears that came. The man looked at Colin, began to shrug his shoulders but stopped, "I didn't see."

"I know that. You didn't see." Colin's voice was hoarse, choked, and his throat burned. He was surprised by the anger in himself.

"Why didn't you tell me…" the man began, but he must have assessed the accident, Colin's twisted face, and determined it wasn't worth his time to appeal to the redhead on the ground crying hot tears. He turned and kept walking, shaking his head a little, maybe as a way to say sorry without admitting belief in a guilt of some kind.

And Colin was crying, twelve inches from the bird who was opening and closing, opening and closing its beak. And then the true injury showed itself, trickling out the right side of the little body; a little trickle of red at first, but soon the blood became pink coils of innards, leaving the silent screaming bird, seeping onto the black asphalt. Then, within the same silence, the bird was finished. And the stillness it had, now, made Colin realize that it hadn't been still at all, before.

Here was a bird that left the nest, jumped out of the nest, for what? Something. A need. And to end this way, it was not fair.

"Why didn't you move?" Colin asked, snot dribbling from his nose.

A few years ago, when Colin was in med school, he was awarded a grant to study health rituals of groups that practiced alternative medicine. He had read about the Radical Faeries in a graduate essay, and was curious about the healing circles, their reiki training, but also the costumes, the flagrant sexuality, the strange mix of rugged outdoorsy-ness and feminine spirituality. Mostly, though, his heart beat faster when he read of their communal living spaces, huddling together for meals and daily rituals. He and two colleagues went out to Starland, one of the Faerie retreats in the Mojave Desert. Colin was taken aback when they first arrived, the compound no more exotic-looking than a meth lab in the middle of a vast expanse of yellow and brown chaparral, a small mangy beige stucco ranch house, right out of a forgotten part of the San Fernando Valley, a shit-brown "Main Hall" no bigger than a living room, a couple banged-up trailers, shed structures, broken gurgling septic system.

The Faeries were all ages and kinds, sixty-year-old men with dyed purple hair, tattooed twenty-somethings with unshaven chests and nose-rings, wearing velvet top hats. One had been a public defender, and thought the constraint of law and the business suit would destroy him, so left his job, his wife, and now walked around the ranch in the nude. They shared rooms, food, chores, everything. They hugged each other in greeting, touched all the time, holding hands as they chatted, or resting arms on shoulders, legs on legs, tousling hair. When they touched Colin, he tensed at first, but became comfortable quickly, even touching back. Though he didn't consider himself a religious man, and had left church when he left Oklahoma, Colin watched the Faeries come together for a moon ritual, whipping streams of fabric around in the air, or to fashion handmade candles for the coming Equinox, and he wanted to join, the presence and warmth of it reminding him of the better moments in Oklahoma, when family came over for Thanksgiving, taking each other's hands during prayer, belonging to each other somehow in the clasp of moist skin, a communion. The Faeries danced after dinner, sang to each other while they hung laundry—even if they had atonal voices—or one night, once again under the moon, they shed their clothes and ran through the dark, and seemed so unafraid, one with a purple feather boa trailing behind his outstretched arms, laughing.

Colin caught himself laughing, too, watching the men, but not in ridicule—like so many of his friends, like Michael would, a cackle in their throats. These weren't gay men like he had ever seen. They weren't reserved, like Colin, shy until he became familiar with what people expected from him. They weren't catty, like many of the men he knew in Los Angeles. What he saw was a fullness, as if their voices, their arms, reached out on all sides of the endless desert, and embraced it. Colin wrung his hands, didn't know what to do with the excitement. He thought of Rio's family, the closeness, the familiarity of them, eating dinner together, touching, Tia grabbing his cheeks, "we're gonna get these fattened up", and Colin wanting her to fulfill that promise, as long as she kept touching him. And these men, their bodies moved to each other's rhythms, much like his own family back home when they'd be performing their own rituals, getting ready for Sunday dinner, or his siblings performing their chores on Saturday mornings, one sweeping, one scrubbing counters, one cleaning out the fridge, so they could watch cartoons. And, maybe even a little like he and Michael, yes. But he and Michael were two bodies, a couple. This was many, a family. A concert of people; messy, but lovely. *This* was lovely. This, he thought, was healthy. He never felt anything so certain before.

Within two days his posture changed. His hips swung more freely, intuitively, in conversations, washing dishes with the group after dinner, walking. He let them dress him up, apply glitter to his eyelids. He didn't think about where his shoulders were, as he usually did. Michael would say, as they brunched on a Santa Monica Boulevard patio, "I can't stand those queens that parade around with their shoulders back, like they're Goddamned Miss America. It's so unnatural. Jesus, be *men*." Colin wondered if any of the barb was meant for him, and quietly looked off, into the sun, to melt the cold feeling. At Starland, the people Colin saw *were* men, he felt it as a warm glow in his gut.

Colin even got naked. The Faeries were gathering in a large hot tub after dinner, and invited Colin and the others to join. Colin said no, at first, looking down, pulling his shirt away from his slight paunch and soft chest, and then immediately felt ashamed of his refusal. He wanted to get in. Was it his Oklahoma modesty? Was it Michael? He looked around—none of the Faeries were perfectly sculpted West Hollywood beefcakes.

Besides, Colin was younger than most of them which, upon having this thought, he felt ashamed again, that he was comparing his virtues to the others. They wouldn't do that, the Faeries didn't care, and that was what he admired so much about them. Just as he was chastising himself for the shallow thoughts, one of the hairy, bear-like Faeries leaned towards him and whispered, "You just gonna stand there, darlin'? We're all beautiful here." With that, Colin pulled his shorts off. The Faeries extended their arms to him with wide smiles, and he dipped his timid body into the pool. They clapped, whistled, and Colin laughed. He looked around at the men. They talked and laughed, comfortable with someone new sharing their home, their hot tub. Colin felt that he, too, was that kind of person, or at least he could be that person. As his body opened to the heat, he relaxed, dipped his shoulders under, closed his eyes, still tingling from the exhilaration, and exhaled. The laughter and conversation softly floated around his head, and he drifted.

He almost thought about nothing for a moment, but then imagined Michael, sneering, laughing at the Faeries, their glitter and randomness, their spirituality. He certainly knew that Michael would never agree with a lifestyle anything close to Starland. Michael didn't even want to live with a roommate. Colin knew it wasn't uncommon, had reservedly accepted Michael's want for them to live alone, had thought it reasonable then. But now the idea seemed selfish, cold, confining. That tight little nest of his life, a small safe place in the world, what Colin thought he wanted—the respectable career, the reliable lover, a future that was visible from the doorways of his cozy apartment—he now realized he confused somehow with his mutual desire for family. It was what he understood to be family, his Oklahoma family, safe and small and tight and safe. And Michael was safe, Michael was true and reliable, and Michael was, in some strange way, like Oklahoma, like all of its safety, and yet Michael was also like Oklahoma in all of its confining restraint.

Colin heaved and opened his eyes. He had left his safe, secure home in Oklahoma to get away from what he couldn't be, and that is exactly what he eventually chose when he got away from it. The heat from the pool started closing in around him, his lungs tightening in the hot steam, the weight of the water pinning his limbs, filling him with panic. He jumped out of the pool before anyone could protest, ran behind the Main Hall, the side that backed to the endless black night of the desert, and caught his breath.

*

At the last dinner before his departure, as the Faeries all held hands for their spirit circle, Colin decided that he would move to Starland. To do this, he would have to leave Los Angeles, and Michael. His hands shook.

He came back, back to their apartment, knowing Michael would be at work, and began furiously stuffing clothes, toiletries, pictures into a suitcase. He knew he had to leave before Michael came home, or he wouldn't go at all. What would he do about school? He wasn't yet finished his pharmacy studies. He would start studying holistic medicine instead. He liked holistic medicine, yes. He grabbed some of his books, ones that he knew he wanted to read again—Thoreau, Emerson, Whitman—the ones that got away from him in college because he didn't know then what he wanted. What about his parents? He would tell them that he missed the country, that he didn't care for the city anymore, which was partially true. So much had gotten away from him in his life, and now that he knew what he wanted—maybe for the first time—he wondered how he could have lived without truly wanting something for so long. He found his camera, stuffed it in the suitcase. And, oh, how beautiful the desert was. Even the few friends he had—that were not Michael's—would understand. He went into the kitchen, snacks for the long drive back to the Mojave. And what about Michael?

What about Michael?

Colin sat down, his right hand clutching the near-full suitcase, and tried to picture Michael, his deep brow, his dark handsome solidity.

Michael didn't cry much, but this would shake him, this would be a seizure. Maybe he should wait for Michael to come home, face-to-face, tell him why. He would have to steel his resolve when he spoke to him. He knew that Michael wouldn't understand, but maybe by sharing his excitement, the discovery of this side of him, the love with which he could say it all, the *certainty*, Michael could accept it. Not at first, sure, but maybe he would grow to accept it, and at least be given the respect. At least that way Colin wouldn't feel like a thief, tearing into their life together, ripping away what they had built, creeping out without regard to years of, what? Happiness? Not exactly. Not exactly, but not nearly, really. Something more than ambivalence, and less than happiness? What would that be? And, was that all bad? Was anyone really happy? And the happiness that he knew at Starland, would that last? Does anything last?

No. Michael wouldn't accept it. And, Colin knew he couldn't face him, either, would never get the words out, with Michael sitting across from him. Michael was strong, knew what he wanted, always—what drew Colin to Michael in the first place—and Colin knew it would be difficult to convince Michael of his desires when there was always a tinge of doubt in his voice, in all that he believed, even this, the most certain he's ever been, but nevertheless a doubt that Michael could detect. Michael would slip his own resolve into that small cleft of Colin's doubt and pull, pull it open until it was fully exposed.

Colin's hand loosened its grip on the suitcase, slowly uncurling, going limp, a thin sheen of sweat quickly evaporating off the plastic. He experienced a stillness he had never known before, sitting in that chair, the weight of his limbs like they were dead, and only his mind alive. Michael loved him. After all he had done for Colin, Michael didn't deserve to be abandoned.

And, by the time Michael came home that evening, everything—the pictures, the toothpaste, the hairbrush, the clothes—was back in place, and he was met with the fresh steam of boiled pasta hiding Colin's face, wafting up along the ceiling and back to the floor, a loop. Michael kissed him on the neck in greeting, and Colin felt the spit like it weighed something, like it was pressing into his flesh, wrapping heavily around his windpipe.

*

Colin stared at the dead pigeon through swollen red, eyes. His curled hands were laying on the sidewalk, forgotten little bowls, still, head slack against his chest. He felt the wet wind of the Pacific that whipped through Golden Gate Park hit his scarf-less neck, that Michael always warned would get cold, even in summer. "Why don't you wear a scarf, Colin? Just wear a scarf. It's common sense." The city came back, the whir of Sunday traffic, songs blurring by in cars, voices and phone calls and openings and closings of doors, coin purses, things. The eucalyptus was crisp and clean in the air. He felt no desire to move, none, on his knees on the edge of the sidewalk, even amidst the movement all around him.

A woman, maybe ten years younger than Colin, noticed him slumped on the sidewalk. Her leggings and army surplus jacket were a little too tight for her, and folds of fat peeked out from her sides, her face soft and round, with a couple speckles of something like paint on her forehead. She knelt down next to him, and said, "Hey, you okay?" She then noticed what Colin's eyes were fixed on, and immediately went over to the dead bird. "Aw, poor thing." She looked back to Colin, who looked at her and then immediately lowered his eyes. She was about to ask him something, maybe if the bird was his, but paused and nodded. She leaned down onto the road, picked the bird up, guts and feathers on her fingers.

Colin watched her, his breath getting bigger, his eyes welling again with tears. She had picked up the bird.

"Was it a car?" she asked.

"A man," Colin barely said.

"A man," she said.

More of the bird's guts wet her hands as she stroked his head. "That sucks. Where did it come from?" She looked around.

Colin shook his head. "It jumped."

"Huh?"

Colin cleared his throat, looked at the girl. She had an oval face, none of her features delicate, a fleshy button nose, full cheeks. She was strong, he thought, she could be alone if she wanted to. "The bird. He didn't know."

She looked up instinctively, to the gray sky, the wires crossing above. "He needs a place, yeah?" She raised her eyebrows in wait, and Colin nodded, but he didn't know what for. A place for what? To rest? A place to rest? Why do we rest the dead? Maybe it was an apology for never getting the chance to rest when alive. He thought of the cemeteries that seemed to belt around the outskirts of Tulsa, their upright, stone monoliths breaking the flat plain of land, a disruption in itself, an apology for life all around the living.

The woman carried it to a rosemary bush that grew against the building behind them, and laid it on the ground. "There," she said, and nonchalantly wiped her bloody hands on the bottom of her jacket. "Hey," she said to Colin. When he looked up to her, she smiled a close-lipped smile, and left to cross the street.

*

At the brunch, celebrating the engagement of their very suitable, very similarly lovely friends, mimosas in hand, Carol followed Colin out the back door, where the sun was beginning to bowl, that very brief moment when a San Francisco backyard enjoys something close to warmth.

"Can you believe it?" she asked.

"Of course I can," Colin said.

They clinked glasses, and Colin swallowed the last of his mimosa.

"You know, I thought you and Michael would beat us to it. I mean, I know it's different," she said, rolling her eyes. "Is that it? You were waiting for it to be legal?"

"That would make it easier," Colin said.

"It's kind of weird. God. I'm happy? You know? It's just kind of weird." Carol fiddled with her hair, rolled her eyes, and laughed a little. "Who would have known I'd be marrying…that I'd be with someone like Max."

"Why?" Colin asked. He squinted in the light, wanted to see her face.

"I don't know. He's so, I don't know. It's not like you and Michael. I wasn't always so sure, you know?"

Colin nodded, keeping his eyes on her. He looked for any sign of insincerity, a crease across her face, a subtle wink, a twitch, a pinch of lip. Nothing. "Sure."

"Somewhere along the way, I realized it's not just about love, you know? It's, it's a lot of things, right?" Carol laughed again, and tucked strands of hair behind her ear.

"Yeah," Colin said.

"You know, we get older."

"Yeah," Colin said.

Carol laughed again, shifted her body more towards the sun, and sighed. "Ah, but you guys are lucky. So lucky." They sat in a slightly unwelcome silence, as if Colin missed his turn to speak, but he was afraid of what he might say. Anything that came out would disrupt her perfect image of his life. What difference did it make, anyway? She clinked his glass, then scrunched her nose. "Oh, no. This," nodding to the empty glass, "cannot happen. Not today. Give me that, I'll be right back."

Colin clasped his hands, and lifted his face to the sunlight, hoping to melt the emerging cold in his gut, that tightening cold, but he knew the sun could never reach down that far.

*

Colin had not moved at all, slumped on the cold asphalt, when Michael strode up with a small box, one previously used for canned green beans. "What are you doing on the ground? Where's the bird?"

"It's dead," Colin said.

"Oh, I thought it..."

Colin shook his head.

"But, where is it?"

"It's gone."

"What, a dead bird, and it's gone?"

Colin swatted in front of his face. There was nothing there, but he felt the need to rid the air of Michael speaking, of ruining the silence, the mourning. "Michael."

"Well," Michael said, extending his hand down to Colin. "Hey, at least you tried. And I got a box."

But Colin knew he hadn't tried. He looked at the dark spot where the bird had been, and thought of the woman that put the bird in the rosemary bush. Colin realized he had only *wanted* to try, and that was the difference. He had not acted. Wanting to act, yes, but failing to. He looked off, for some light to come into him. *Oh my*, he thought. He ran his fingers through his thinning, golden-peach hair.

"Colin, you all right?"

Colin, still on the ground, shook his head.

Michael didn't lean down. He instead put his hand on Colin's shoulder, and looked around.

"Hey. Come on. Let's go home."

Colin shook his head, and that was all. He wasn't yet ready to look into Michael's face, not yet fortified enough to look him directly in the eyes with the refusal. There was still doubt, but he knew he had to, that there was no other way, and this time he would. He would. Wouldn't he?

BEEN CUT

Mason stood at the riverbank and watched his father's back over the water. The small love handles pinched hard at his sides, bent down like he was, and looked like cheese melting out of a burger bun. His father dropped his head and let out a tight, clipped grunt, probably a muffled curse word, and that meant the crawdad trap was gone again. The silver of the early morning river cast his father in silhouette, the bank itself not yet catching light. No boats on the river, still a little chilly on the Sacramento Delta, even in the middle of summer.

His father turned. "Rope's been cut, for sure." Mason couldn't make out his face, but could see the string dangling from his fisted hand. "It's no accident."

"Maybe it's a boat coming through, cutting the line."

"No boat coming this close to shore, Mason. You know that."

"Maybe the critters gotten smart, and used their claws for a change." He waited for his father to snort—or, better yet, laugh—like he used to. Mason loved to make his dad laugh, would work hard for the reedy cackle that betrayed his deep voice and barrel chest, that made him and his brother giggle, and his mother, too, when she was still here.

"Don't be dumb, Mason," his father said, his face taking on a dog-like look when angry. "Some son-of-a-bitch is stealing from us. That could have been supper."

"We could make another, Pop," Mason said. "It's just some apple juice jugs and a fish head."

"You gonna buy those jugs?" his father asked. He looked beyond Mason down the river bank. Noah was making his way over, his flip-flops on his hands like mittens.

"What's going on," asked Noah, his voice barely audible over the soft movement of water.

"Your big brother here is making light that someone is stealing our crawdad traps for themselves."

Mason stood up straight, then thought better of it and relaxed his shoulders some. "We don't know someone is stealing, Pop. Who'd wanna steal a plastic crawdad trap?"

His father licked his lips. "For the crawdads, knucklehead."

Noah stayed quiet, looking at his father, then Mason, and shrugged.

"Let me see the line," said Mason.

"Be my guest, big man," his father said, and tossed it over. Sure enough, the line looked cut, just like the last time.

"Maybe the trap is still down there. Didn't you weigh it down?"

His father climbed up the bank and toward the trailer, which was a quarter mile down the road leading away from the river. "Why don't you see for yourself? I gotta go to work, anyhow." He hard-smacked a cluster of low-hanging sycamore leaves, and disappeared beyond the rise.

"You know it's not in there," Noah said, pointing to the river bank. "Why would someone cut the line and leave the trap down there?"

"Shut up, Noah." And even though he knew his brother was right, Mason got into the water calf deep and began feeling along the bottom. Waste a little time. He wanted to wait til his father left for work before he went back to the trailer. He wasn't afraid of his father, but it pained him to see the scowl he wore, more and more often these past two years, since his mother left. At first it was just drinking himself to sleep and once in a while getting foul over small things that never used to bother him—co-workers running late to the dock, hungover from a wild night at the Flamingo Lounge, or an unusually light catch that made him little money, or Noah walking into the trailer with muddy shoes. These days, it seemed everything bothered him. Just better to stay out of his way.

"Even if it was left there, the current would take it once the line been cut."

Mason looked up from the bank. Noah stood there, lightly swaying his arms akimbo back and forth, his sandy waves needing a haircut. The clouds were marbled, the high sky almost the silver of the water. Not the best day to go swimming, get burned up quick. And their best friend was at a Bible Study camp somewhere beyond Lake Folsom and wouldn't be back until next week. Mason thought maybe he and his brother could make a new crawdad trap, surprise their father. They could walk over to the El Rancho Grande Market and ask Rogelio, the owner, if he had any empty apple juice jugs. Mason knew how to make the traps, and he could teach Noah, who was only seven, but was old enough to learn it, too. It was pretty simple. And Mason was crafty. When his mother was still around, they'd go into the market, or one of the bait shops, and look for knick-knacks, to make them into something else. All around the trailer were wind chimes made of bolts and fishing line, wreaths made of flies and tackle. "I wanted to be an artist when I was a little girl," Mason's mother always told her boys while she glued washers into geometric patterns on coffee mugs. Mason missed those evenings at the kitchen table. His mother, Mason and Noah made gifts for Christmas, and his father sat with them, pressing his finger in a knot when needed, calling her Martha Stewart, laughing.

He knew it had to be a thief, but Mason couldn't figure out why anyone would want to. Most people in town who had the taste for crawdads owned their own fancy metal traps that caught dozens of them in one overnight drop. If Mason's dad was lucky the jug trap caught five or six, maybe eight. And, there were plenty of dads in the water right now. The rice paddies were draining, and it was deep summer. You could catch the things just by disturbing the bank and scooping one in a bucket, even catch them with your bare hands. Things were dumb as the rock they crawled under.

Town was a good hour's walk, so Mason told Noah to get on his sneakers. They'd take the East Levee Road around the bend. The sloughs were full of boats this time of year. By the time they dropped down into Rogelio's parking lot, the sun was fully high and it was hot. There were a half dozen trucks parked outside, a pretty busy day. A couple guys were catching shade under the aluminum porch awning, the white paint almost clear peeled off.

Rogelio saw them walk in first thing. "Boys. Where's your Dad at? He needing something?"

"No, sir," Mason said. "He's at work."

Rogelio looked out the window. The silver hair on his temples bright against the black, shiny in the light. "Well, I bet he's not fishing in the Bay today. Bound to burn up with this sun."

"You have any big jugs, Rogelio?" asked Mason. "Those ones you sell apple juice in?"

Rogelio pointed out to the small, cramped store. "Aisle two, down there. I think we have some."

"No sir, I mean used jugs. Empty. We're gonna build a crawdad trap."

"Oh, I see. Still doing those plastic deals, yeah? I don't have none right now, but I'll hold 'em for you if I get any. Better be careful with those. Game and Fish'll fine your Dad if he's caught."

Mason looked down at the peeling linoleum, and asked where else he might find something similar, for the time being.

Rogelio's moustache pushed up to his nose as the man thought.

"Try the gas station. Bet you could make yourself a trap with oil or antifreeze jugs, something like that. Bound to be empty ones at a gas station. What happened to your old trap, or you just making more?"

Mason told Rogelio about the cut lines while Noah looked at the wall of gummy candies.

"You'd have to be mean or desperate to cut someone's jug trap. That's downright ornery. Probably some stupid kids. Maybe those Pinckney boys. They'd do something like that. Damn kids, breaking windows, throwing trash in the river. They close by you, right? Yeah, just down the way, right? You ask them?"

The Pinckneys lived in a single-wide below the West levee. There were five kids and their mother, DeAnn, and sometimes a man would be in the picture, now and then. The oldest boy, Turk, somewhere around seventeen, tall and skinny and red-headed like the rest of them, was already in jail, and Bobby, the second oldest, got kicked out of school last spring. He and one of the sisters got in trouble for busting out some windows in the Hidden Harbor Marina a couple months ago. Mason's mother would tell him to mind his P's and Q's around those kids. She'd say, "They are probably just fine down inside, but things get rotten on the outside first, so be mindful."

Mason and Noah did score at the gas station, and went back home with two antifreeze jugs and a Clorox bottle. Their father would bring home bait that evening, and they'd drop a new trap that night.

While eating Taco Bell that his father brought back from Rio Vista, Mason asked whether Rogelio's suggestion might be a right one.

"The fucking Pinckneys," his dad said, and swigged on the last beer of his six-pack. "Only so much trash would fuck with a man's shit like that, little bit that he has."

Noah spoke up, "I don't think it was them, Pop. None of them been around this way in a while. And Tammy's nice. She wouldn't cut our lines."

Their father snorted. "Might be nice now, cuz she's young, Noah. But not for long. All women grow spiteful. And hell, with a mother like that," and pulled the rest of his beer with a long swallow. Everyone in town knew that Pinckney himself left after he caught DeAnn cheating with another fisherman from Walker Landing. Since then, DeAnn and the kids always got looks when seen around town. Mason knew what DeAnn did was wrong, but he felt sad whenever he saw her and the kids.

His father opened the fridge to grab a beer, only to find none left. "Fuck," he muttered, and slammed the door. "Besides, Noah, how they know it's our traps they fucking with? That doesn't make sense. It's not personal. They just rotten kids doing rotten shit." He tapped his fingers against his temple. "You gotta make sense, Noah."

Noah stared at the Taco Bell wrappers.

"I'll be back soon," Mason's father said. Within thirty seconds the truck was revved and throwing dust on the road.

Their father usually went to Striper Bar or the Flamingo these nights. He'd get home after Mason tucked Noah into bed; but Mason was still awake, listening to his father's heavy body moving in the dark. The door, the keys on the counter, the footsteps to the back room. It was becoming more and more frequent, twice, three times a week. Some things set it off. A bad catch, a late notice in the mail, any mention of their mother, which they learned to keep in their mouths. And now, the crawdad traps.

The first time Mason remembered his father coming home drunk was just before his mother left, those months they were fighting. Mason and Noah hid in Mason's room, listening behind the door. Their mother was speaking softly, but their father was yelling, tears in his voice. Who is he? Who is he? Their mother's firm voice insisted the boys would hear, but their father said, "If you leave, don't think you can come back and say hi to them whenever you feel like it."

"It's not always about another man, Ben. That's just it," she said, but their father had already crashed through the door into the night.

The next morning the line had been cut, again. It was their father's day off, so he drove the boys into town, to make sure Isleton knew about the criminal stealing Ben Parker's crawdad traps. "The best place to spread the word be Hap's Bait & Tackle," which had a bulletin board filled with flyers: a school bake sale, day labor, a found Labrador. Right as Mason walked in he remembered a time when all four of them came to the shop, just before his mother left, maybe the last time they all were there together. His father was rummaging the shelves, probably seeking some mechanical bit for his Spinfisher. His mother stood with her arms folded in the middle of the aisle. She said, "A bunch of worms," real low, under her breath, but loud enough to hear, like she was talking to the wall. His father, half-listening, muttered, "Indeed, that's what they sell," and kept on searching for whatever he came to get. His father hadn't noticed that his mother was then glaring at his bent-over frame, surrounded by the plastic flies and fishing wire. Mason remembered feeling like an alarm went off inside his head, and he was about to tug on his mother's arm, to either get her attention or to take it away. Before he could do this, her eyes went from something mean to something shut off, like her brain suddenly wasn't attached to them anymore. He decided to leave that face alone, and slunk into the tackle box and river map aisle with Noah.

Hap was at the counter when the three of them walked up. "Hey Ben. You bring your young men in, I see."

"Yeah, it's been a while, I guess."

"Well, I see your ass almost every damn day." Hap laughed, grinning at the boys. "Nice to see some good-looking folks in here, for a change."

"Somedays."

Hap leaned over the counter down to Noah, like he was going to share a secret. "You must have gotten your good looks from your mama," and winked.

Noah looked startled, then turned to look up at Mason. Mason nodded to him, and Noah roamed over into the aisles with live bait.

His father pointed to the bulletin board next to Hap. "Say, Hap, could I post something?"

"Sure, Ben. What you selling?"

"Nothing like that," his father said, and told Hap about the crawdad traps.

"And you sure it ain't being cut by a propeller or something?

"Three times, Hap? And no propeller's getting that close to shore. Besides, this is a clean cut to the line. Propeller cut would be all mangled."

"True that," said Hap. "You thinking some punk kids, or something."

"Don't know, but someone's having a nice crawdad boil as we speak."

"So, you want to put up a flyer about your missing crawdad traps."

"Well, it's not so much the traps—they're just jug traps."

"Jug traps!? You shitting me, Ben!?" Hap's laugh made him lurch forward and cough. "I thought maybe someone stole a couple steel ones. Hell, those jug traps ain't worth the paper you waste writing up a notice. Why don't you just make some new traps and drop them in?"

Mason's father was chewing the inside of his lip. "Why, so they can just be cut again?"

Hap rose his hands up in appeasement. "Son, why not drop the damn things in another spot along the river and be done with it?"

Mason's father's mouth tensed up even more. "That's not it, Hap. It's the principle of the thing."

Hap slowly nodded, cleared his throat, reached to the small desk behind him, and turned back with a red Sharpie and a piece of scrap paper. "Alright, Ben. Make sure you leave a number, in case someone sees something out of sorts."

When they got back to the trailer, Mason and Noah went straight to work on rigging a new trap. "It'll be the best one yet," said Noah.

"It's no good if it's stolen," their father said.

"Maybe Hap's right, Pop. We can drop it at the spot off Tyler Island Road. No one would notice it there."

His father stared at his boys, then walked over to the fridge and grabbed a beer. Mason focused on the trap, didn't want to see his father gulp his beer while staring at the wall.

Mason and Noah were almost finished when their father suddenly popped up from the table, grabbed his keys. "We need to go make a neighborly visit."

*

DeAnn opened the door to the trailer before Mason's father even got up the front steps. She was wearing an oversized t-shirt that said "Valley Girl" in black and pink bubble letters. Tammy, only a bit younger than Noah, was next to her. She waved, and Noah smiled. Her youngest son, Danny, was on the other side, shirtless and barefoot, with a fruit roll-up in his hand.

The Pinckneys were what most people would call the Parkers' neighbors, even though they lived more than a mile down the road and on the other side of the levee. Mason's father mostly saw DeAnn at the Striper trying to get the men to buy her vodka cranberries. She would proudly tell people that she was from Sacramento, though she arrived in the Delta with Bill Pinckney when she was barely fifteen. At first she worked at the front desk of the B & W Resort Marina, where they rented pontoon boats and day-runners, but something happened between her and the boss that no one ever got the full story on, and DeAnn only said "a man playing the victim, like always," whenever people asked her. Rumor was she now collected disability, but no one knew for what. She was a pretty woman, somewhere in there, but standing on the porch anyone would swear she was fifty, though she couldn't be older than thirty-five. Mason's father touched the brim of his baseball cap.

DeAnn leaned on the doorframe. "What did I do now?"

"Hey DeAnn."

She looked at Mason's father, then down at Mason and Noah. Her mouth curled a little at the ends and her eyes softened a bit. Then, she looked back at his father. "Well, Ben, I assume this isn't friendly."

"Someone's been messing with my crawdad traps down at the bank." He didn't make any accusation, but might as well have.

"What do you mean, mess with?"

"Been cutting the line, stealing the trap."

DeAnn slowly closed her eyes and sighed. "And what you asking me about it for?" The words were soft and had no tone to them, like she'd said them before many times.

"It's happened three times, so it's no accident."

"And you think it's me? One of my kids?"

Mason's father looked down, rubbed his hands on his pants. "Well, someone's been cutting the lines."

"Ben, have you been drinking?"

"It isn't no boat propeller, I'll tell you."

"Now that you got all liquid courage you're gonna come accuse my kids of stealing your crappy traps?"

"We know some of what your boys do, DeAnn."

"Well, you're sharp as a tack, aren't you? No shit. I'm still paying for those windows down at the marina. But none of 'em are here, anymore. Danny and Tammy are the only ones at home, now."

Mason's father looked at Danny, who was still eating his fruit roll-up.

DeAnn followed his eyes. "Christ Almighty. Serious?" And like she was making a choice right then, DeAnn grabbed Danny's shoulder and swung him to face her. "You been stealing goddamned crawdad traps, Danny?"

Danny's eyes got wide and he leaned back from his mother's sudden fury, shaking his head.

"This man seems to think you did."

Mason's father put his hands up a bit. "Now, I don't know..."

"You stealing traps, Danny? Tell me!" Without even a second for Danny to answer, DeAnn's hand whipped across his face with a loud thwack. Danny didn't cry out, but held his cheek with both hands and clenched his jaw. Tammy ran to her brother without a sound, grabbed his hand, and pulled him into the dark of the trailer.

DeAnn looked up to Mason's father. "There. Make you feel better?" She glanced just for a moment at Noah, and it seemed her eyes got a bit soft again. "What you really angry for, Ben?" And she closed the door.

When his father started the truck, he suddenly slammed his hands on the steering wheel three times. Noah's eyes got big and he backed against the passenger door. Mason touched his knee. When his father's breathing slowed, he said, "Your mother used to hang out with that woman back when she was running around on Bill Pinckney. Could say she was helping her in such a time." He said nothing else the rest of the way home. When they pulled up to the trailer, he told Mason to mind his brother. "I'll be back soon."

The next evening, Mason made dinner, Valu Time turkey pot pies with mustard, and frozen peas. They all ate in silence. After, their father drank beers while Mason and Noah worked on finishing the new crawdad trap. They punched holes and twisted garbage ties into where the two jug tops were cut and aligned. The antifreeze containers weren't as flush as the apple jugs, but it looked like it would work just fine. Mason showed their work to his father.

He stared at the trap. "Why the fuck you still fiddling with those?"

The boys were silent.

"Really? What for, Mason?"

"Cuz you want to catch some crawdads. To boil them for dinner."

His father stood up. "Have we had any for dinner yet? Have we?"

Mason shook his head. Noah ran to his room.

"And why haven't we, Mason?"

Mason swallowed. "Cuz the line been cut."

"So, why keep on making them?"

Mason barely shrugged his shoulders, almost afraid to.

"You know what they say? Insanity doing the same thing thinking you'll get different results."

Mason looked up at his father.

"Are you insane, Mason?"

He knew he shouldn't say anything, but the image of DeAnn Pinckney's pink hand across Danny's face had stayed hooked in his mind. The moment her hand and his face met kept playing over and over again.

"It's not me and Noah's fault, you know."

His father's face changed, from Doberman-like to wide all over, and his hands suddenly looked empty. He walked to his keys and out the door. When Mason heard the truck start, he went and sat at Noah's bedroom door, and listened.

On the day their mother left, she took Mason and Noah to the Spindrift Diner, their favorite. She watched them devour their burgers and milkshakes, would run her fingers through their hair, touch their hands and faces. Mason figured something was about to happen. And then she told them she was moving to Denver, Colorado.

"Where is Denver?" Noah asked, barely five then.

"It's far, but not too far. In the mountains."

"Why can't we all go?" asked Noah.

"Well, sweetie, your Daddy wants to stay. And, your mama needs a break, is all. Just for a time."

"Will you visit us?"

Mason's mother sucked in a quick little breath, and forced a smile. "I sure hope so. We gotta get your Daddy open to the idea."

"Can we visit you in the mountains?"

"They are big and beautiful," she said.

"Why?" Mason asked.

His mother's smile dropped, and she looked in the space between her boys, a spot on the plastic booth. "Because the mountains are as far away from Delta as I can get. While I got time." Her eyes got glassy and it looked like she tried to get the smile back, but she pulled her lips into her mouth instead. Mason didn't know what she meant by having time, but he knew she meant it, that she had already left, in a way.

Mason's eyes adjusted quickly to the dark, though the moon was low and little. He chose a spot behind a stand of young white alders, around the corner from the bank where he had dropped the crawdad trap, where it disappeared into the murky water. He figured he wouldn't be spotted, even if the culprit was looking around for possible ambush. Mason knew he wasn't going to ambush anybody. He only wanted to know who was doing it; and if it was just some punk kids, as Hap called it, then maybe spook them from doing it anymore. He had nothing to ambush with, anyway.

But what if it was someone that wouldn't oblige so fast as to run off upon being found out? Or, what if they noticed Mason watching them, and didn't take too kindly to it? Mason looked up at the grouping of stars above the tree-line. He would need to have a plan, just in case. He gathered some rocks and stowed them behind his hiding spot. If someone did come by tonight, he'd throw the rock so that it landed on the other side from where he was staking out, just to startle and throw off the thief. That would get most people running without him being found out. Sitting in the alder stand, he felt good, like he was doing the right thing, and it was all his choosing. Whatever Mason could do to take the anger out of his father, he needed to do. He leaned back on one of the trunks and counted the small burls pressing against his skin.

Mason didn't even realize he'd dozed off until he heard the rustling in the grass coming from over by the riverbank. The thief may have even walked right by him, for all he knew. He squinted to see, made sure the dark wasn't playing tricks on him. But he was too far away from the bank. So, he listened. Grass, clicking of disturbed rocks, and feet in water. He was sure of it. His visitor had come. He grabbed one of the bigger rocks and heaved it in the direction of the sound, of his antifreeze jug crawdad trap, into the dark. The rock hit soft mud on the bank with a dull but loud thud. Then, Mason waited. No sound, except for crickets and frogs.

He decided to throw another rock. This one went farther and it splashed into the river. With that, footsteps moved fast, running, away from the bank, and right onto the dirt road that led back to the East Levee Road into town, and to their trailer, and right past where Mason was hiding. His heart was pushing blood fast and hard into his head, making a sound of its own. He gripped one more rock in his hand, squeezed it against his thigh and bent lower into the branches. The figure came around the bend with slapping steps, like running in flip-flops, pale skin and a steak knife catching only instances of the low moonlight. Mason slowly rose up, the rock still in his hand. The grip loosened. He walked out onto the road before Noah ran past him, his little brother looking behind as he clapped up the dirt, and then turning forward.

Noah halted, about a room away from Mason. He did not try to speak or keep running, even when Mason slowly made his way over to him. When he was face-to-face with Noah, Mason looked out to the river, and dropped the rock.

"Did you cut the line before I got to you?"

Noah shook his head.

Mason nodded. "Does it look like anyone messed with it?"

Noah shrugged his shoulders. Mason put his hand on his brother's neck and steered him back down to the river bank. They made sure there was no sign of the knife on the line. They also checked the jug, which already had one decent sized dad trapped inside.

Mason said, "Dumb ass things." He dropped the trap back in the water. They walked back home in silence.

"You gonna tell Pop?" Noah asked, just before the trailer appeared in the clearing.

Mason looked back to the river, little glints like knives in the light, and sighed. "You know you can't do that no more, right?"

Noah nodded his head.

Mason met his eyes. "I mean it. No more."

Noah offered his pinky finger, and Mason linked it with his own.

"I miss her," Noah said.

Mason looked at the trailer for a bit, then back, and brushed the hair from Noah's eyes.

"C'mon, then. We can't wake up Pop."

Mason watched Noah walk into the front door of the trailer until the dark insides swallowed him, then sat in the rusty lawn chair facing the road. He sat there, for how long he could not say, but he waited until he knew there would be no crying coming out of him. After a while the stars had moved along the sky and the moon entirely faded, until the treetops in the East glowed purple, and everything else began finding its shape again.

AIN'T NO THING

This is a story of violence.

The MUNI bus lurches forward, enough to rock Richard from his afternoon stupor. Purses slump, an expensive coffee paints a woman's white blouse the color of dirt.

"Thought it was an earthquake," someone says, to no one in particular.

MUNI continues the thin metallic wheeze on its rise and fall along Market Street. With rain done for the day, the sky opens up, a single shard of light falling across Richard's lap through the window. The heat soaks through his creased black slacks.

Richard knows that the bus wouldn't lurch in an earthquake. He knows if there happened to be one, it would feel more like a bumpy road, more like riding over a deeply-grooved grate. It might even lull riders to sleep. And, with all of the vehicle's superstructure, it's probably one of the safest places to be when a big one comes along, the rubber of the tires somewhat absorbing the seismic wave.

When did he learn that? Sixth grade. Earth science kept him transfixed to the overhead projections that Miss Sims slid onto the light box with a grace and ease that made her his favorite, the confusion of kindness and pubescent lust. How he tingled with the possibility of her unbuttoned collar. *This is what the Earth looks like, under the surface.*

Richard shakes. This comes from deep within his body, from some hypocenter nestled in the layers of muscle and bone and blood, a signal of sorts. He needs something. Perhaps it is hunger, or something of comfort, the chenille blanket he drapes over himself while watching TV on the couch, even when he is not cold. The rippling of this knowledge intrigues him, the want beginning as impulse that quickly surges through like a wave, until the moment he ultimately gets whatever it is his body thinks it needs. Then, all better. A shake, a quench, then all better. He's been wondering what he needs, but can never satisfy his body with an answer. Loss fills his stomach with a viscera, of regret, an emotion of the gut. The weight of it is unspecific.

He thought his arrival to San Francisco was the first exact moment of his life, a pure fulfilling of need, when there was no toil of choice. He was a seismologist, he loved the arts, and always felt calmer by the ocean, and Caroline would be with him. When he was offered the position with the California Department of Conservation, Mines and Geology division, he immediately accepted. A needle to the groove of the perfect song. He took long walks around Nashville to give the city a proper good-bye, but was overcome with how much he didn't feel he belonged there. The streets were whizzing with cars, but empty. Bicentennial Park was emerald green in the day, its faux-Parthenon looming dramatically from its low rise, but empty. He walked into his favorite bar in Hillsboro, a dark friendly spot where he'd spent many nights after graduate seminars chatting about sediment, marriage proposals, liquefaction. He ordered his usual Stella. The barrel-chested bartender didn't recognize him, but smiled anyway. Richard didn't know anyone in the bar. He finished his beer quickly. It was time to go. He wasn't quite twenty-nine. He and Caroline packed everything they had into a ten foot UHaul, newly married, and drove West.

Caroline was excited to move to San Francisco, the sophistication of it. She thought Nashville—where she had lived her whole life—was so, she would say, catatonic. She always referred to the people and the city that way. "We are better than this hillbilly town." Her hair would shake around her face, as if conviction alone could make hair shake. Richard would tilt his head softly, take her hand and caress the lines of her palm to calm her. He would excuse the small cruelty of her judgment as a requisite flaw to an otherwise exquisite creature.

The weeks that followed their move appeared more resolute to Richard. The air was clearer, as if he could feel each atom entering his lungs. The scent of things became more distinct, and didn't swamp together the way they did in the languid Southern air. Colors popped, felt outlined, like in a grade-school coloring book. The feel of his fingers on jersey gave him an erection, and his love-making with Caroline was adolescent. He marveled at their thighs pressed together, her softness to his knotted muscle, her fine, almost red hairs to his coarse black. Richard felt the molecules of his reality become more crystalized. He decided then that happiness made itself evident in these moments of sensual clarity, that happiness was somehow bound in this visceral shift in perception. All sounds, his favorite song.

He isn't quite thirty-five.

Three young men enter the bus and sit across from Richard. They wear the baggy jeans that fall well below their asses, a fad that baffles him, particularly for how long it has been a fad, considering fashion's whimsical attention since the likes of E Network and TMZ. One of the boys has scraggly, dirty blond hair, while the other two have loose fros. Richard can see their boxer shorts thankfully cover what their pants can't. He wonders what holds up the jeans, and if this trend among young men is supposed to signify having a big cock, one big enough to act as a hanging knob, of sorts. A clothing fad has to come from somewhere. He thinks to look this up on the Internet when he gets home.

They have come on the bus with paper bags of spicy chicken wings. Richard can smell the spice, that tickle in his nostril, then his throat, where taste and smell blur. He would love to take one of those wings, to feel the security of the meat in his own mouth. He realizes now that he is indeed shaking because he is hungry. He recalls the last time he had a proper meal—yesterday morning. By the time he gets home, however, he will walk in to the quiet, empty apartment, Caroline's clothes missing from the closet, and regret will fill his belly again. Whiskey will be dinner.

The boys begin to eat. Richard wonders if Miss Sims ate chicken wings. Miss Sims was black, the only black teacher he ever had. Her voice was smooth, that of honey being poured into a large bowl, ribboning at the bottom before disappearing into the liquid mound, his memory of that voice the stuff of adult fantasies in his teens, teen fantasies in his adulthood. He would sometimes lay that voice over the shrill of the few women that actually made it to his bed, the ones before Caroline.

An earthquake, class, is what happens when two blocks of the Earth suddenly slip past one another. The surface where they slip is called the fault. The spot where the earthquake really starts is called the hypocenter, buried deep below the surface, unseen. The epicenter is the spot that we can see, but is not the source of the earthquake.

The boys inhale the wings with flourish, almost a highly conscious, theatrical exaggeration. They take a wing, shove all but a sliver of bone into their mouths, and suck the meat off, lips pulled back to reveal gristle and teeth. The sound of the slurp fills the bus, or at least it seems like that to Richard, who watches them out of the corner of his eye while pretending to gaze out the window. He can see the boy across from him, through the reflection, crane his head up and thrust the wing behind his teeth, and suck. Lips smacking, a kind of sex sound, really (maybe the kind he and Caroline had made, when their bodies were still new). And then the chew—open mouthed, the meat churning round his tongue, which wags to catch renegade bits of chicken, another kind of force. An animal sound, something wild, a bear behind a wall. It repulses Richard, the sheer uncivilized nature of the suck and gnaw.

After the boy has ripped the bone of flesh—ligament, cartilage, everything—without so much as a hesitation he drops it, not back in the bag but in the tight space between his seat and the window. Richard is shocked, flabbergasted, appalled. The bone pitifully lolls on the floor. The ease in which the boy does this fills Richard with heat, an embarrassment, not necessarily for himself but for the bus, for the people riding, maybe the city, all of humanity, he's not sure. It's definitely the same kind of heat he felt the first time Caroline subtly refused his hand, walking along the Embarcadero on a surprisingly warm evening, not too long ago. Maybe a year, two years ago? Had it been that long? He wanted to bring her to romance, to feel it all around her, to feel it with him. The Embarcadero was a perfect idea. He pulled her out of their flat, her protests feeble enough, but she had been silent the entire ride on the train, staring out at nothing, and certainly not looking at him. Once there, Richard felt hopeful, with the briny scent of the Bay. As they walked, passing restaurants and piers, cyclers and coffee stands, he slipped his hand into hers, and just as smoothly she pulled hers away, and walked ahead silently. They had been married only a few years. This wasn't supposed to happen. The weight of the refusal had him follow behind for several minutes, his face flushed with a cold fire that didn't have a source, a locus to identify, so he could fix it, put it out. All he could do was watch her figure, his hands balling to fists, and feel the pounding of his own steps on the concrete walk. It scared him that he imagined running up behind her and pushing her into the Bay, pushing her hard against her back, to send the refusal from his refused hand to her rigid body. When she finally turned around and said, "I'm hungry," he sucked in a grateful breath and replied, "Let's check out one of these seafood places."

Richard thinks to ask why the boy on the bus has done this careless act. The lack of hesitation is what throws him, as if it was impulsive to drop the chicken wing, not a choice at all. It appears to Richard that the boy wasn't doing it out of protest, or of a need to demonstrate utter distaste for San Francisco public transit—this pure, inherent lack of consideration. Where did this boy grow up, Richard wonders, probably in the *ghetto*. Richard would italicize ghetto, because it is a foreign word, and all foreign words are italicized. *Project housing*, with weeds splitting concrete playgrounds, *graffiti* narrating a lost cause. Maybe the boy still lives there, perhaps somewhere in *Oakland*. Probably didn't have a good female role model growing up, he thinks. Has no family unit. Maybe he even sells drugs. Maybe he has been harassed by the SFPD so much and for so long that he feels like the city doesn't care about him, so why would he care about the city, and certainly this MUNI bus? Maybe the feeling is so deeply rooted in him that dropping the bone willy-nilly is as impulsive as instinct. No matter how Richard considers it, though, he feels the heat in his face and his hands ball into fists.

When Richard first saw Caroline on the quad, the sun was trapped in her strawberry blonde hair, her whole being: teeth, skin and light. All nuance and detail were smoothed by the humid morning. And, in the distance, how could he not fall in love? He was still exhilarated by his presence at Vanderbilt. Nashville had been the far reaches of his world—so far from West Virginia, his family, his small shotgun clapboard cottage on the edges of a small town nestled in hills that felt huge to Richard then, insurmountable. He perhaps had wanted to fling himself farther than Nashville, but everything beyond those West Virginia hills felt like frontier. The frontier is different for everybody, and unless you're willing to go into the unknown, you settle for the edge of knowing.

He did not approach Caroline quite then. He brought her a flower—

not a rose, or lily. Richard picked flowers for girls, because he knew it was thoughtful and that it somehow kept a dying institution alive, but afterwards felt guilty taking a life for the uncertain promise of another. He modified the task to buttercups, wild daisies, thistle, in this case a fallen magnolia blossom. Caroline found him refreshing, a true Southern gentlemen, not the chest-beating bravura of Nashville's gentry that she was used to, and told him so.

Many girls had said this to him, that he was gentle. Every time, his ears grew hot. So, this is what perplexed Richard: the women in his life adored him, initially, always tilting their head with something sweet he said—and meant!—or when he prepared a surprise picnic in the park, or a surprise birthday party, or a surprise gift in between the pillows. By the end, however, the women in his life despised him, and for what? He did not stop saying sweet things to them. He maintained the level of surprise; if anything, the surprises became more surprising, more elaborate, with more effort. When he began to see that his gestures were met with something other than the light he always sought to ignite, he worked harder, consulted friends, family, became more complex in his designs to elate them. "Oh, Richard," his mother would say, almost cupping his soft, pale face in her hands through the phone, with a bitterness in the honey that Richard never understood.

One night, shortly after his senior prom, April Garrett was crying in the car, parked in front of the dark ribbon of the Kanawha River, where they, on occasion, made out in the dark. Richard didn't understand. He had just given her a bracelet. It had charms dangling from it—a dancing bear, a Coca-Cola bottle, a garnet heart—really popular at the time. She opened the box, and for a long moment kept her head down, her hair falling in her hands.

After what seemed a full minute of silence, he ventured, "Do you like it?"

And she growled. Low at first, a guttural, ugly sound, but it grew higher and higher until it was clearly sobbing, but an angry kind. Her face emerged from her hair. "Why did you get me this?!"

Startled, Richard's wide mouth hung long. His blue eyes, large, Kewpie doll-like, opened wide, full of surprise and love. April had seen this face, this utter sincerity, many times, too many times, had fallen in love with this face, before. He knew that she was cheating on him, with Clay Goodall, one of the junior football players. It wasn't a secret, everyone knew. She pulled Clay into a back room during a party the weekend before, in fact. Richard was there, knew what was happening, even in his drunken, slurred reality. He grew angry—a paralyzed version, anyway—slumped against a couch where a couple had passed out, his stare fixed on the long hallway into which she had disappeared. But, he was afraid to do anything, afraid that opening the door that hid April and Clay would make the act more real, not the dulled unfocused thing that it was. He didn't say anything, even after she emerged from the hallway, everything about her tousled, her body fiercely electric and ready to fight, her eyes locking with his intently, waiting, or even later, when he drove her home. Instead, he thought to buy her the bracelet. He thought that if he proved how much he cared for her—that he really cared for her—she would choose him.

In the dark interior of the car, she raised her hand to his temple. There was a fairly deep gash, barely-healing, purple and brown, running right to his hairline, his black curls feebly concealing. "And, what about this?"

"It's nothing," he said.

"Your father."

"It's nothing." He tried to take her hand, to comfort her.

With that, she threw herself out of the car, and began to storm off.

"What is wrong?" he yelled after her.

April writhed in her sundress, her slender arms punching the empty space around her. "You don't get it, Richard!"

"Get what?"

"You give me this stuff, all this stuff. And your head. And you tell me it's nothing. And...I get angry. And...I want you...to *want* something from me!"

"I *do* want you."

"No, from me. *From* me. I never feel good enough, Richard. And that sucks."

Richard felt lost in the words, the simple sounds of them, and it all seemed silly to be arguing over emphasis. Of course he felt she was good enough. Didn't he want to celebrate how much she was to him, by buying her things like the bracelet? "April, please be reasonable."

She threw the box and bracelet into the river with a shrill grunt, took a few steps, turned back in shame, perhaps indecision, for just a moment, and then walked into the dark, away from him, for good. He didn't know whether to stare at the spot in the river where the box had disappeared, or where April had. The heat came into him, the fury, the want to transmit the fury. He clenched his fists, fixed his stare on the black river until it cooled the burn in his face.

On the bus, another wing, another sucking, schlurping, and the boy absently drops another bone, same as before. Richard looks around to see if anyone else notices. If they do, no one acknowledges. He snorts. No matter how bad this kid had it, there still is no reason for such thoughtlessness. It's not Richard's fault the kid grew up in project housing. No one on the bus oppressed this kid. Who was he to take it out on them, these people riding the bus just like him? They weren't that different, all being transported to wherever they need to be. The bus was a place of equality, Richard thought, and he was even surprised by his discovery. Yeah, he prided, the bus was a place of equality. It didn't know economic circumstance, didn't know *race*. Of all places for these boys to be discourteous, why here? Richard snorts again, loud, but not so loud to seem directed at anything specific, though he wants to. Who knows what this boy is capable of? Maybe he even has a gun, or a knife. You can never be sure in a city. Richard wants to say, "Direct your frustration with your life to the proper channels—your parents, racists, your parole officer. Not us."

Caroline says Richard has bad eating habits. She says he takes too much time cutting his meat, chewing his meat. Eats like a bird. Constantly coos and compliments her food. Rakes the fork along his teeth slowly and "ooh"s. Makes her shiver. She turns her head and rolls her eyes in this way that brings the heat to his face, usually at dinner in mid-description of his uneventful day. Well, if only she could see *this* guy, he thinks.

Caroline has left him, is seeing someone else. Caroline claims that she and Richard have grown apart. He doesn't really understand what that means. He doesn't think of marriage as ever growing together. He sees it more as a parallelism, moving in the same direction, but never explicitly joining. Sometimes, when two forces move jointly, they are not always flush, he knows that. They can drift, open up, only then to realign. Isn't that better than coming together, better than colliding? Nothing joins together without something of a collision. There are always faults.

The boy drops another bone into the crevice with a small thud. Richard feels helpless. He thinks, how can everyone watch this happen? Of course they see it. How can anyone miss this grotesque display, these punks eating like pigs, with no regard? They speak to one another, about the wings or something else, Richard is unsure, because all he can make out are a series of mumbles. No wonder they are pigs, slobs; they can't even speak English. Everything failed them—their families, their neighborhood, now their education. This is what gives *black* people a bad name, Richard thinks. He thinks about the handful of black friends he has had over the years. He bets they would be embarrassed, watching these boys act with so much irreverence. He's certain they would be just as angry as he is, at the pure irreverence, at the animal in these boys on display, while everyone else on the bus is keeping their animal inside, like civilized people, for the common good. He wishes that one of his black friends were on the bus right now, to let these boys have it, to really have it.

Richard was a graceful boy all during puberty. He didn't have an awkward growth spurt, and his frame filled itself steadily. The pimples never came in torrent, but spaced themselves out to one here and one there. With his hair curling softly, darkening to mahogany, and his already large blue eyes, Jessica Hawkins took him for hers by the end of lunch on the first day of seventh grade. Richard was enchanted by the affection, and would dress up for school every day—creased pants, button-up white shirt, loafers. She would see him in the morning, tilt her head, "Oh, Richard," grab his hand and walk into the schoolhouse.

He knew what beauty was, saw the many images of Jesus on posters, Warner Sallman's *Head of Christ* hanging in the portico of his small white-steepled church, his pale face looking upwards into the light, the gentle loveliness, and tried to do the same for Jessica. As his voice grew deeper, Richard affected it to sound lighter, breathier, more ephemeral. He insisted to his mother he must grow his hair long. His father, a coal miner who worked the Upper Big Branch, worried that he was going to be a sissy-boy, and pleaded with his mother to "cut the nonsense." Richard saw his father as the antithesis of beauty, coming home blackened by coal, streaked with sweat lines, bulky. Black and bulky. His father muttered, hocked snot and spit in public, belched at the dinner table. Richard saw the way his mother looked at his father, like something that needed to be fixed. Richard washed himself more frequently, brushed lint off his clothes every morning. His father would look across the room, and shake his head, something sad in the face. Richard entered school and tried to float across the linoleum hallways to avoid making a sound—heel-ball-toe, lift, heel-ball-toe, lift—sliding his clean hand into Jessica's with the gravity of a feather.

After two weeks of going steady, she pulled away, in disgust. "What's wrong with you?"

Caroline was worried they didn't fight. She thought it odd, that instead of a passionate argument with equally passionate reconciliation, they merely "talked about it," then sat silent across the dinner table, polite and reasonable, the sole sound of fork to porcelain. Richard urged that this was what civilized people did, what sane people did. There is no end and beginning, only a continuance of things, and harmony is more real than resolve. Easier. Caroline would slowly shake her head, and look out the window, so still, the lines of her face tugging gently. "Richard, it's all right to be angry." Richard believed that one day Caroline would discover that it wasn't okay to be angry, that he was being virtuous, this harmony that he worked so hard to cultivate, that if more of their contemporaries acted with the same logic and reason—these wonderfully civilized traits mankind could harness—there would be less suffering, less conflict. Caroline was smart; he was confident she would come around, discover this noble truth he held so deep and sure.

But instead, she packed up her life, and left with a sorrowful apology—a false resolve, he thought. And he has to admit: he was furious. How could she be so blind, that leaving is not a true resolution, that she only upset the balance of her life, as well as his? How could she let another guy fuck her, slip his cock up inside her, open up her flesh, make her feel ecstasy and love, and be fooled that the orgasm was the beginning of something better? Richard used to make her feel that, always tried to make her feel that. And knowing some other man was doing this brought about the hot gnash in his face. He revealed none of this, though. It was rash, emotional fury, and ultimately the expression of human weakness. Lesser men, uneducated men, expressed this animal instinct, and it led to violence, abuse, crime, oppression, misogyny. When energy builds, beyond the friction of its jagged edges, it breaks out, it breaks, he knew that. He enveloped the fury, clutched it, and, with reason, slung it back down into the deeper parts of himself.

He had made Caroline happy once, he was sure—it had been his favorite thing, especially when he could get her shoulders to rock with the deep, throaty laugh that defied the thinness of her. She'd toss her head, her fine red hair sliding along her back, mouth wide and full of tidy, straight teeth. He loved this. When they had just gotten married—he still in grad school—and moved into their first apartment together, he caught her several times worrying over finances. Caroline had never known struggle, he knew that, not like his family had. Once, he caught her staring into the empty space that should have been a dining room. They could not afford a table, having used all their resources for the wedding and the move West. Richard was heartbroken at the worry, the thinning and quiver of her lips. "What are we going to do, Richard?" Later that evening, she walked in from work to see him seated in that same room, wearing his one suit. He had taken a moving box, covered it with a bed sheet, candles, picked flowers and a bottle of cheap white wine. Draped on a folding chair was her favorite dress—the blue jersey sleeveless V-neck that fell on her hips in a way that made her want to move them. He asked her if she wouldn't mind dressing more appropriately for their date. When she came back from the bedroom, supper was served: mac and cheese with chopped mushrooms, flickering candlelight, and a grinning Richard. She laughed. Afterward, he put on some Dinah Washington, and danced with her in the small room, speaking to her with a horrible French accent, kissing along her freckled arms, from fingertips to elbow. She laughed, her head, her hair, tilted back. Happy.

The first time Caroline came home late, he wasn't concerned. It had been a warm day for San Francisco, and he knew Caroline relished those days, maybe even missed the balmy nights of Tennessee, and believed her when she said she wanted to walk home from work. She lingered around the kitchen as he finished preparing dinner, and he asked her "You hungry? I could make you some fish."

She widened her stance. "But you're making pasta."

"I could head back to the market."

She snorted and said, "Jesus," whipped off her belt, and disappeared into the bathroom. The sound of the shower felt like a wall to Richard.

There were other times that Caroline wanted Richard to know, he can see that now. She told him a few months ago that she was going to see her sister back in Nashville for the weekend, but no plane ticket ever appeared on the credit card statement. Richard took care of all the bills. Caroline knew that. Later that month he mentioned to her before bed that he hadn't seen a charge. She said, "What do you make of that, Richard?" She stood in front of him in her negligee, arms crossed. The heat came into his face. He wanted to accuse her, call her a liar. But he forced open his hands that had balled into fists, knew these thoughts to be irrational. He instead said, "You look beautiful." She dropped her head down, only said "Well," and slumped into bed.

Maybe he did know that she was fucking some other guy. Maybe he simply wanted to trust her, trust that the woman he loved would do right by him. Besides, if she was fucking some other guy, what could Richard do? It was up to her to stop, not him. It wasn't *his* fault.

She didn't stop.

The boy has done it again, dropped another chicken bone onto the floor—*ain't no thing*—and this time Richard is certain that this boy, and all of them, are true, real, thugs. So what if the system failed them? That doesn't mean one needs to thwart all decency. Richard flushes vividly, and he feels his lips snarl over his bleached teeth. These kids are his imbalance, the scourge of humanity that the rest—the thoughtful, the well-intended, the contributors—have to support, so that the whole system doesn't collapse. And this is how they pay back, by sucking on a fucking chicken bone and tossing it to the floor, that working people's taxes paid for. That *Richard's* taxes paid for.

Richard wants to grab that chicken bone. He wants to pull it off the floor with one quick surge of his body and rake the thing across the boy's face. He wants to grip the bone in his fist and run the sharpest edge through the boy's neck. All of them. He wants to stab their necks, watch their eyes grow wide as their blood geysers from their arrogant necks. He wants them to look helplessly at the chicken bone, half-drenched in red, then at Richard's face, and realize their folly, their misdeed, that they are the ones that make good, decent people like Richard angry.

Richard feels the heat all over his head, but especially in his ears, imagines little flames flickering at the tips. And he knows he needs to quell this anger. Anger upsets the balance. He would get to this point after Caroline would go on and on about the same complaints, the failure she saw in him. Where was his passion? Where was his manhood? Him, getting redder and redder. "Grow a dick, for once, Richard." He would have to walk out of their flat, run down the stairs and step out into the dark San Francisco cooling, walk until the heat left. When returned, certain he could continue the discussion more reasonably, she had given up, retreated into a defeated silence that confused him.

He needs to do the same now, to walk out, into the chill, to quell the fire, but just as he is about to pull the cord, to request a stop, the boys rise. When the bus stops, they exit, but not before the boy, the one sitting across from Richard, the one who dropped the wings on the floor, tosses the whole BBQ-soaked bag behind him, it plopping in the aisle next to Richard's feet.

The first woman to break his heart was Krissy Montier. Richard had taken one of his mother's rings and presented it to Krissy at recess. He debated it all morning, staring at his mother's jewelry box, trying to prioritize the act of generosity over the sin of thievery. He told Krissy that his feelings were real. We all know that life is just as serious, then, as it is, now. Krissy took the ring, examined the bold opal, the thick band, too big for her thumb. "It's ugly," she said, and tossed it behind her as she ran to the tetherball court.

Richard ran off, too mortified to go back into class. He realized he couldn't go home, either. So, he walked along the river, careful to walk the side opposite of town, and waited until his mother would expect him. When he sidled up to the house, his mother was at the screen door. Her robust body near took up the doorframe, and seemed even larger because her arms were propped against the screen. She had been crying. "I'm gonna have to tell your daddy" is all she said.

Richard wet himself from the beating, and for two days he couldn't sit flat in his chair at school. His mother chopped vegetables, near slamming the knife to wood while the belt snapped across her only son's body, could hear her husband explaining the beating while he did it. "Because of. a. girl? You. some. kind of. pansy? Dammit, Dickie." He was crying, too. Richard's father had a ferocious love for his boy, and beat him for wrongs with equal ferocity. Richard's mother conceded in these times, while gripping the sides of her dress, that love and violence were indistinguishable when men, like Richard's father, lived and worked in the dark.

That same week, Richard received his first D, in English. He had been crying in the shabby sandy courtyard of the schoolhouse. Miss Sims noticed, came over and gracefully sat down. He showed her the report card. Miss Sims tilted her head to the side and said, "Oh, Richard," and assured him it wouldn't be that bad. Richard looked at her, really looked at her, perhaps the first time ever with an adult, with nothing but what he had, and her conciliatory smile faded. After a moment, she simply slipped her dark hand into his pink hand, with the gravity of a feather, and they stayed there silent for quite a while, both looking out over the Kentucky blue-grass, rustling in the soon-summer wind.

Richard stares at the bag, smeared orange and white, dirty, crumpled, limply balled, and he can't help but sense the giant failure, all around, in this bag. This bag, and everything failing. The people on the bus are looking into nothing but the picture of their own failures, their jaws slack, their faces pulled down. But Richard stares. He stares at the bag, the tossed bag. Caroline looked at him the same, like a greasy bag. Caroline. Caroline takes her hand, smears it into the grease, and rubs it on a cock—not Richard's cock—and slides herself onto it, and laughs directly at Richard as she bobs up and down on this cock, as she gets fucked by someone not Richard. He burns the stare, wet and hot, and everything blurs around the bag, his eyes fire, two tight balls of heat, imploding stars. There is a tight, white burn in his gut, a bigger one than ever, something pushing inside him, a pressure that has nowhere else to go. Richard hears his teeth grind against each other.

A young woman sitting in a seat near Richard leans towards him, her crisp blue business suit straining in the thighs. "Are you alright, sir?" she asks, her eyebrows creased in concern.

The question is a portal of sorts, the pressure, and Richard immediately pulls his gaze from the bag to the woman. His hands implode into fists. "Bitch." He doesn't dare look directly at her face, Caroline's face, her face, a woman's. He imagines her head bleeding, almost the color of BBQ sauce. "Bitch." Her hair splays out of the neat bun almost in ripples, slathers and clumps with the blood, and the BBQ sauce, too. Over and over, head to floor, he imagines his hands gripping her, slamming her. He can feel it. Head to floor, head to floor. Caroline, how could you? "You bitch." Over and over.

A girl next to the young woman screams, and Richard starts. He feels the temperature drop, and the rest of the bus comes into view. His shirt pulls with sweat, curls clomped to his head, so much hot water in his eyes, now looking at the woman's face, which is wide open with fear, her body slowly backing away. He yelps out apologies or promises, but not in a language anyone, including him, understands. *I am the center of things,* he thinks, *there is a world on all sides.*

Bodies turn, and an assortment of men jump from their seats, ready to do the thing men do to make things right. The bus driver has already stopped the bus, moving to the back, and everyone is looking at Richard, who is shaking, perhaps shivering, Richard can't tell. He can't look at them, their faces full of disgust, and instead looks down at the floor, the chicken bones, and now his shoulders lurch forward, and he cries, large, heavy sobs, curls himself into the bus seat, knees to his chest, his face pressed against the window, the resolute lines of the city blurring with the fog of his breath.

AFTERWARDS: THE STORY OF EVERY LIVING THING

Structures—big *things*—are making me panic lately. Large, beyond-the-size-of-human things that we dwell in, that we swarm inside, that we rely on to stay intact. Made by us. Every time I bike or drive or walk over the Golden Gate Bridge, I can't help but marvel how this 85-year-old thing stands in the water so confidently. Why doesn't this crashing wild water erode the foundation to the point of collapse? I ask this to my roommate, Sean, who prides himself on his physics knowledge, even though he is a photographer for hipster hoodrats in the Lower Haight. We are driving over the Golden Gate with our friend Marie to get Dippin' Dots in Sausalito.

Well, eventually it will fall. I mean, it *is* water, he says.

Exactly, I say. Look at what it does to earth, to metal, to skin.

Nothing is indestructible, he says.

Then, why do we drive on this thing?

Why are you asking this while we are on the bridge, Marie asks.

The bartender at The Page and a tremor (un)plant the idea. I am sipping my pilsner, the hiccup of earth occurs, and debris from the ceiling dusts the floor. I look up. Everything looks the same. Large brick slabs nestle between lines of concrete mortar. I look at her, and she's shaking her head. I share the empirical probability that if shakes like this happen enough, the ceiling could fall—*the sky is falling, the sky is falling.* She laughs, and then stops laughing. Wow, that's deep, she says.

Why? I ask. Her eyes stay fixed on the ceiling.

It ends, man. You know? It ends with the nothingness that, like, when the whatever that was whatever has finally ceased, you know, being what it was, and becomes many things, or many parts of things. Or maybe it's nothing at all. You want another beer?

I stare at the ceiling with her.

It begins with the observations, quick glimpses, interstitial musings that bob now and then, when the air isn't too hot or cold, when the spaces between our doings aren't busy swatting away bugs from our face, yelling at drivers who cut us off, pushing ourselves into the world with a force that could never be mistaken as listening. A woman is talking on her cell phone during her lunch break. Her panini sits patiently as she pulls a strand of loose hair, fiddles and releases it into the wind. The hair dances nervously, snakes in its weightlessness, then settles on the back of a chair filled with a man who is talking on his cell phone during his lunch break. He doesn't have much hair left. But he does pull on his nose. He smears the crusty mucous, some on his creased slacks, some on the edge of the table. He misses his mother, who passed away the previous September. He is considered attractive by several people. So is the woman. She has already forgotten about her strand of hair, but it has only begun.

In the bathroom after school. I am burning paper because it is punk rock. Trying to convince Chris Curtis that we were supposed to join our bodies in splendid oneness, I watched the fire pare the white paper into gray ash, then fall, disappear out of sight, wondering where it went. Where was this nothingness and suchness?

I was watching the mini-series adaptation of *Angels in America* (I had read the play, and loved it immensely, more than the mini-series, but then is *not* when I got a boner, and that is what this is about.) The actor playing Louis says to the actor playing Mormon Joe that smelling some*thing* is the particles of the object coming into you. The object—that very real thing—sloughs off bits of itself at all moments, every moment, a little bit and a little bit. Upon hearing this I get an astonishing boner.

Making out with Karen Fiorito in the tenth grade, I unexpectedly got a nose bleed. She didn't care, even laughed, while my tongue was licking the back of her teeth. Afterwards, after the wetness had dried on her skin and panties, she recoiled at the thin brown line down her neck. I touched it. Where it was dry, it rubbed off and disappeared.

My father opens his hands and says nothing when I ask him why he is my father, why I am his son, the vastness of the question in my small five-year-old mouth. He sits on the porch, the wicker chair, facing the stretch of Blue Ridge woods that was infinite to me then, even though the road ran 100 meters beyond. The question feels authentic, but I can feel its danger. I stare at his hands, my chest barely higher than his lap. Even then, I know something abides in the open hands—a fullness, a thing, the answer I seek? We open our hands, something goes. What?

Sausalito eases itself within the final breath before the Headlands exhale into the Bay. We pass the storefronts designed for white people who vacation by eating. The Dippin' Dots cart is next to a *rest*aurant that rests itself over the water, perched on a pier, a series of exposed wood beams disappearing into the murky water. Barnacles grow all over the wood.

See, look at that, I say. Isn't everyone freaking out about that building relying on *wood in water*? I mean, isn't it soaking, softening, rotting?

Well, yeah, I guess, says Marie.

Then, I say.

Eventually, my roommate says.

Then what? I say.

Then, they build another one that won't rot for a while, he says.

I ball my fists and shake, and let out a contained growl, only for them.

Dippin' Dots! Marie says, and runs along the pier towards the cart.

One week after we shared a bed, you looked at me from across the car that shielded you from my barbed questions. Your eyes showed that you had rubbed me off, and I disappeared from you: the mucous, the semen, the spit, the hair, the particles of me, all gone. Where did it go? If it is a gift, who have I given it to, now? Do I have any say in this?

I stare at my brick ceiling—when will it corrupt enough to give up and fall on my face while I sleep? How many shakes will it take?

We made the Titanic, we made the Hindenburg, we made the Challenger Shuttle. We made Fukushima. We make love.

I am a structure. Dust is skin, floating in the light. When we sleep, we not only shut off the waking world, we dissipate, pieces of us leaving, rolling in the soft motion, in stillness. Air and water move around us, taking bit by bit. We stand, and we can hold up many things, and we are certain, even as the little bit and the little bit leave. How many shakes will I take? And what of the violence?

When I was small, a fierce and tight little bud of my eventual self, my grandmother swayed with the stories of every living thing. The late summer would swarm with dandelions, and when they were ready, the white fluffy seeds would take flight. The flower knew of its end, and would let go in one last grateful gesture of life, a soft woolen sigh into the air. And off the seeds would go, twilling with the air and light. I chased them, delighted when they grazed my outstretched palm, but I had no desire to fold my fist around them, and they'd take flight again. My grandmother looked off, beyond me and the seeds, over the horizon and somewhere beyond. It was a face I couldn't have understood. My father opens his hands and says nothing when I ask him why he is my father.

One last grateful gesture of the mystery, and why it should stay that way. The world breathes, in its own woven way.

We are sitting on the dock, Marie, my roommate, and I, facing the Bay on a sunny day. Below us, the water. We are supported by rotting beams of wood. We are nibbling our Dippin' Dots—nibbling renegade flakes of skin, sea water, salt, early morning sneezes, fingernail crud, snot, rust, cat hair, dog dander, fly eggs, cum, sweat, pus, shit, fish ick, toe jam, rotten meat, fungus.

This is fucking good, my roommate says, little bits of Dots sticking to his hipster whiskers. Marie is too busy tonguing the dots to say anything at all.

Yeah, it is, I say.

ACKNOWLEDGEMENTS

Stories from this collection have appeared in the following publications:

The North American Review: "Babies"
Barrelhouse: "Been Cut"
The Greensboro Review: "Clips"
Callisto: "The Story of Every Living Thing"
New Millennium Writings: "Growl"
Fourteen Hills Review: "Coffee Spilled"
The East Bay Review: "Gethsemane"
Offbeat Anthology: "Saving a Bird"
Saints and Sinners Anthology: "Jingle-Jingle-Pop"
StoryQuarterly: "Ain't No Thing"

"Growl" is the winner of New Millennium Fiction Prize
"Coffee Spilled" is the winner of the Oregon Writers Colony Award
"Clips" was a finalist for the James Knudsen Fiction Prize, the Curt Johnson Fiction Prize, the Meyerson Fiction Prize and the Robert Watson Fiction Prize
"Saving a Bird" was a finalist for the Saints and Sinners Fiction Prize

"Jingle-Jingle-Pop" was a finalist for the Yemassee Fiction Prize & the Saints and Sinners Fiction Prize
"Babies" was a finalist for the New South Fiction Prize
"Ain't No Thing" was a finalist for the Alexander Cappon Prize

The Violence Almanac was a finalist for the St. Lawrence Book Award
The Violence Almanac was a finalist for the Robert C Jones Book Prize
The Violence Almanac was a finalist for the Prairie Schooner Book Prize
The Violence Almanac was a finalist for the Grace Paley Prize for Fiction
The Violence Almanac was a finalist for the Many Voices Project Prize
The Violence Almanac was a finalist for the Santa Fe Writers Project Book Award

Thank you to Lambda Literary, Ragdale, Shuffle and the Hub City Writers Project, for granting me the space and support to write these stories.

To Diane Goettel for her grace and enthusiasm with this collection. What a treat to work with you.

To the dedicated teachers and readers of these stories in their many incarnations: Randall Kenan, D.A. Powell, Doug Kearney, Maxine Chernoff, ZZ Packer, Robert Glück, Junse Kim, Chanan Tigay, Peter Gadol, Kazim Ali, Dan Chaon, Janet Sarbanes, Irwan bin Iskak, Toni Mirosevich, Shobha Rao, Angela Leroux-Lindsey, Andy Sean Greer, Chad Koch, Katrin Gibb, Kendra Schynert, Carson Beker, Jennifer Lewis, Juli Delgado Lopera, Sarah Broderick, Ari Moskowitz and Monique Mero-Williams. Thank you all for your generosity and support.

The family and friends who have helped shape me. I am grateful for you all.

And Marco.

MIAH JEFFRA is author of *The Fabulous Ekphrastic Fantastic!*, *The First Church of What's Happening*, and co-editor, with Arisa White and Monique Mero-Williams, of the anthology *Home is Where You Queer Your Heart*. Miah is a founding editor of Whiting Award-winning queer literary collaborative Foglifter Press, and teaches writing and anti-racist studies at Santa Clara University. Originally from Baltimore, Miah currently lives in San Francisco.